The Thirteenth Bell

Stories From The Channel

R. D. Thorne

Table of Contents

Prologue

Lowmere was a town wrapped in fog. It curled in from the sea at dawn and never truly left, clinging to the leaning houses and narrow lanes as if the town itself feared to be seen. Even in daylight, Lowmere wore a gray veil. By night, the fog thickened into something heavier, something that carried whispers.

Every child in Lowmere grew up with the same warning: Never count the bells on a New Moon night. The older ones spoke it with a shiver, as though uttering the words too clearly might summon the sound itself. Doors were barred, lamps dimmed, and not a single soul dared cross the cobblestones after sundown. For when the thirteenth bell tolled, the night would claim someone.

The superstition was older than the town itself, passed down through mothers' hushed lullabies and fishermen's muttered tales. They said that centuries ago, when storms battered the coast and ships were swallowed by the waves, Lowmere's people begged the sea for mercy. And the sea answered, though not in the manner they had hoped. Out of the fog came Malrik, a figure caught between life and death, neither man nor ghost, with a bell that tolled from nowhere and everywhere at once.

He offered a bargain. Calm seas in exchange for a life each New Moon. Desperate and afraid, the people agreed. They built their homes in the shelter of the cliffs, raised their children by the tide, and every month surrendered one of their own. Some vanished from their beds, some from the pier, others in the middle of the square. The bell cared not who. It only took.

At first, the bargain seemed bearable. No more shipwrecks. No more floods sweeping through the streets. But as the years wore on, the silence of the missing grew heavier than storms ever had. Families were left with nothing but salt and ash upon their doorsteps. Names carved into stones that none dared visit. Empty chairs that remained empty forevermore.

The thirteenth bell became Lowmere's heartbeat. Slow, dreadful, and impossible to escape.

The lighthouse on the cliff watched it all. Once, its beam had guided sailors to safety, cutting through fog and storm. But as the curse spread, the light faltered. The glass dulled, the flame sputtered, and the lighthouse became less a guide and more a sentinel. People whispered that within its walls lay a relic called The Channel, carved from dark wood and etched with strange symbols. They said it could speak to the vanished, carrying voices across the thin veil between worlds. Few believed such stories openly. But everyone avoided the lighthouse all the same.

On this New Moon night, fog pressed so thick over Lowmere that the sea could not be seen even from the shore. The streets lay deserted. The square stood empty, save for the old bell tower rusting at its center. Its iron mouth gaped silently in the dark, waiting.

The first bell tolled.

The sound was low, deep, a vibration that seemed to travel through stone and bone alike. A second followed. Then a third. Behind shuttered windows, townsfolk pressed their hands to their ears. They prayed the sound would pass them by, that it would move toward another door.

Seven. Eight. Nine.

A dog howled in the distance, silenced quickly by its master. Children were drawn close under thin quilts. None dared speak. None dared breathe.

Ten. Eleven. Twelve.

The silence stretched, unbearable. For a heartbeat, it felt as though perhaps this time the curse had been forgotten, that Malrik had turned his gaze elsewhere. But then it came. Low and final.

Thirteen.

The bell's cry rolled over the rooftops, down the cliffs, across the restless sea. It was not loud, but it was inescapable, a sound that lived inside the chest long after the air had gone still.

Somewhere in Lowmere, a door swung open. By dawn, another name would be spoken in hushed voices, another family draped in grief. The bell's toll had been paid. But not everyone vanished.

On the edge of town, beyond the cobbled streets and clustered homes, a single cottage clung to the cliffs. Its garden was wild, choked with salt-tough weeds, its windows clouded with sea-stained glass. Inside, a girl stood alone at her window, staring out into the fog.

Her name was Ada. Fourteen now, though most remembered her as the child who should not have lived.

Years ago, when she was but seven, the bell had tolled for her. Her parents had clutched her small hand, certain it would be the last time. The town had waited for the morning ash, whispering their pity. But dawn came, and Ada was still there. Alive. Unmarked, at least until the next day, when a faint outline bloomed upon her arm. A bell, etched into her skin like a shadow left behind.

The mark made her a survivor. It also made her cursed.

Ever since, the townsfolk had looked upon her differently. Some crossed themselves when she passed. Others spat over their shoulders. A few muttered that she had stolen another's fate, that her survival had doomed them instead. Children were pulled away from her, doors closed at her approach, and even friends grew scarce.

But the bell never forgot her. Each New Moon, Ada listened to its toll as though it were counting down to her once more. She pressed her sleeve lower, covering the pale mark, but the weight of it was always there. A reminder. A promise.

Tonight, as the thirteenth bell faded into silence, Ada did not flinch. She stood at her window, hand pressed against the glass, staring at the distant glow of the lighthouse. Its beam flickered once, weak and strange, as if answering her gaze. For a moment, she thought she heard voices carried in the fog. Thin, whispering, almost calling her name.

Her heart quickened. She knew what the others did not. That survival was not an end. It was a thread, pulling her toward something darker. She was bound to the bell, to the vanished, to whatever shadow lingered beyond the fog. And deep inside, though she tried to deny it, Ada felt that one day it would call her again.

The night closed in around Lowmere, heavy with salt and silence. Another family wept behind shuttered doors. Another chair would be empty by morning. And on the cliff, Ada lifted her marked arm to the window, watching the pale outline catch the faint glow of the lighthouse. The thirteenth bell had tolled, but the curse was far from finished.

It was only waiting.

Chapter 1:

Toll of the Curse

The echoes of the thirteenth bell had barely faded when Ada heard the screaming.

She pressed closer to her window, her breath fogging the cold glass. Through the thick fog that blanketed Lowmere, she could see lights flickering in the distance. Lanterns bobbed through the streets like fireflies, voices calling out in panic and desperation.

"Tam! Tam Fletcher!"

The name carried on the wind, and Ada's heart clenched. She knew that voice. Mrs. Fletcher, the baker's wife, who always smelled of flour and cinnamon. Her hands were always dusted with white powder from her work, and she had a way of smiling that made even the sourest customers soften. Her son Tam was sixteen, barely older than Ada herself. He had kind eyes and a quiet smile, and he was one of the few people in town who still offered her a nod when their paths crossed.

Just the week past, she had seen him mending fishing nets by the harbor with his father. He had looked up from his work and given her that same quiet smile, even raising his hand in greeting. The gesture had warmed her more than she cared to admit. In a town where most people avoided her gaze, such simple kindness felt like a gift.

Ada's hands trembled as she pulled on her coat. The screaming outside was growing more frantic, more desperate. She could hear other voices joining Mrs. Fletcher's now, calling Tam's name into the fog as if their voices alone could bring him back.

She took her coat from the hook by the door and stepped outside. The fog was so thick she could barely see her own garden gate. The air was heavy with moisture and salt, clinging to her skin and hair like cold fingers. She could hear the commotion growing louder in the town square, but the fog made everything sound distorted and strange. Voices seemed to come from everywhere and nowhere at once.

Kito appeared beside her as if materializing from the mist itself. The brown hyena never strayed far from Ada's cottage, especially on New Moon nights. His amber eyes seemed to glow in the darkness, reflecting what little light filtered through the fog. He was larger than any hyena had a right to be, his shoulders reaching nearly to Ada's waist, and his presence always made her feel safer. The townspeople feared him, crossing themselves and muttering about dark omens when they saw him, but Ada had never felt anything but comfort from his company.

He pressed close to her side as they made their way down the narrow path toward town. The cobblestones were slick with moisture, and Ada had to move carefully to avoid slipping. The fog seemed to part before them in strange ways, revealing glimpses of the chaos ahead before closing in again.

The sounds grew clearer as they approached the town center. She could hear doors slamming, footsteps running across cobblestones, and underneath it all was the sound of Mrs. Fletcher weeping. It was a raw, broken sound that made Ada's chest ache.

By the time Ada reached the town square, a crowd had gathered around the Fletcher house. The building sat on the corner of Market Street, its windows usually warm with lamplight and the smell of fresh bread drifting from its kitchen. Now those same windows blazed with harsh lantern light, and the smell of yeast and flour had been replaced by something else. Something that made Ada's stomach turn.

She hung back in the shadows between two houses, pulling her hood up to hide her face. The crowd was larger than she had expected. It seemed as though half the town had emerged from their locked and shuttered houses, drawn by the commotion. Through the gaps between bodies, she could see Mr. Fletcher standing in his doorway. His face was pale and stricken, and his usually steady hands shook as he held a lantern high above his head.

Mrs. Fletcher was on her knees before the house, her hands pressed to the cobblestones. Her nightgown was soaked through from the fog, and her graying hair hung loose around her shoulders. In the circle of light cast by the lanterns, Ada could see what had captured her attention: A small pile of salt and ash marked the spot where Tam had last stood, the only trace left of the baker's son.

"He was just here," Mrs. Fletcher sobbed, her voice cracking with grief. "He was standing right here, watching for the bell to finish. Said he wished to see if the stories were true, if something truly happened on the thirteenth toll. And then it came and he just... he just..."

"Vanished," someone finished quietly. "Like all the rest."

The crowd pressed closer, their faces grim in the lantern light. Ada recognized most of them. There was old Mr. Carven, who ran the fish market, and his wife, Sarah, who sold herbs and remedies. There was young Tom Whitmore, who worked at the docks. People she had known her entire life, who had once smiled at her and included her in their conversations. Now they looked upon the pile of salt and ash with the same expression of helpless terror that had marked every New Moon night for as long as anyone could remember.

"Poor boy," whispered Mrs. Carven, wrapping her shawl tighter around her shoulders. Her voice was thick with unshed tears. "Such a sweet lad. Always helped his mother with the bread deliveries, never asked for payment when folk were short of coin."

"Sixteen years of age," added Mr. Birch, shaking his grizzled head. The old fisherman's weathered hands were clenched into fists at his sides. "His whole life ahead of him. Was planning to wed the Hartwell girl come spring."

Ada felt sick. She had not known of Tam and Mary Hartwell. The girl was barely fifteen, with copper hair and freckles scattered across her nose like stars. She would be devastated.

"This must stop," said a voice from the back of the crowd. Ada could not see who spoke, but she recognized the desperation in the tone. "How many more are we to lose before someone does something?"

The crowd murmured agreement, but Ada noticed how their voices stayed low, as if they feared being overheard. None wished to anger the curse by speaking too boldly about ending it. The fear was too deeply rooted, passed down through generations like a family heirloom none wanted but could not bear to discard.

"What can we do?" Mrs. Carven asked, her voice barely above a whisper. "The bargain was made long before any of us were born. We are bound to it whether we like it or not."

"There must be something," Mr. Fletcher said, his voice hoarse. "Some way to fight back. I shall not lose my son for naught."

But even as he spoke, Ada could see the defeat in his posture. They all felt it, the weight of centuries pressing down upon their shoulders. The curse was older than their grandparents' grandparents, woven into the very foundation of their town.

"Perhaps we should ask the marked girl," someone said, and Ada felt ice form in her stomach. The voice came from somewhere in the middle of the crowd, but she could not identify the speaker. "She is the only one who has ever survived. Perhaps she knows something the rest of us do not."

"Where is she, I wonder?" Mrs. Carven looked around the square, her red-rimmed eyes searching the crowd. "Strange that she is not here, is it not? Almost as if she knew what was coming."

Ada pulled her hood lower, trying to blend into the shadows between the houses, but it was too late. A young woman at the edge of the crowd spotted her and pointed with a trembling finger.

"There! There she is!"

All heads turned toward Ada, and she felt the weight of their stares like stones pressing down upon her chest. The crowd parted as people stepped away from her, creating a wide circle of empty space around her feet. The silence stretched out, broken only by Mrs. Fletcher's quiet sobs and the distant sound of waves against the rocks.

"Well, well," Mrs. Carven said, her voice sharp with grief and anger. "The cursed child decides to show herself after all."

Ada wished to run, but her feet felt rooted to the cobblestones. She could see the accusation in their faces, the suspicion that had been growing stronger with each passing year. Seven years since she should have died, and seven years of watching others take her place. Seven years of their neighbors and friends and family members turning to salt and ash while she remained untouched.

"Strange thing," Mr. Birch said slowly, his weathered face creased with thought. "How the bell keeps taking young ones of late. The children. The unmarried. Those with their whole lives still to live."

"Used to be more random," agreed Mrs. Carven. "Old folk, middle-aged, it mattered not. But these past few years..."

"Almost as if it makes up for lost time," added someone else. "Making up for the one it missed."

The implication hung heavy in the fog-thick air. Ada felt her cheeks burn with shame and anger. They were blaming her again, just as they always did. As if her survival seven years ago had somehow upset the balance, as if the curse now demanded extra payment to make up for her escape.

Mrs. Fletcher looked up from her pile of salt and ash, her face streaked with tears and twisted with grief. When she saw Ada, her expression hardened into something cold and terrible. "You," she whispered, her voice like the scrape of metal against stone. "This should have been you."

The words struck Ada like a physical blow. She stumbled backward, but the crowd had closed in around her without her noticing, trapping her in their circle of anger and grief. Lanterns cast dancing shadows across their faces, making them look like strangers, like creatures from some fevered dream.

"Seven years," Mrs. Fletcher continued, rising to her feet with the slow, deliberate movements of someone barely keeping control of their rage. "Seven years since you cheated death, and how many good people have died in your place? How many children have turned to ash while you walk free?"

Ada's throat felt tight, as if invisible hands were squeezing it closed. "I never asked for this," she managed to say, her voice barely above a whisper. "I never wished for anyone to die."

"But they did all the same," Mrs. Carven snapped, stepping closer. Her usually kind face was transformed by grief into something harsh and unforgiving. "They died so you could live. My nephew Thomas died so you could live. The Hartwell twins died so you could live. And now Tam Fletcher is gone, all because the curse is still hungry for what it lost."

"That is not true," Ada said, but her voice wavered. Deep down, in the darkest corner of her heart, she sometimes wondered if they were right. If her survival had somehow cursed the town to lose more people than it should have.

"Is it not?" Mr. Birch asked, his pale eyes boring into hers. "Eighty-four souls taken since your night, girl. I have been counting. Eighty-four people who should still be walking among us if the natural order had not been disturbed."

Ada felt tears burning behind her eyes, but she refused to let them fall. Not here. Not in front of them. She had learned long ago that tears only made them angrier, as if her grief were an insult to theirs.

"I am not responsible for the curse," she said, trying to make her voice stronger. "I did not make the bargain with Malrik. That happened centuries before I was born."

"But you are part of it now," said a voice from the crowd. Ada could not see who spoke, but the words carried the weight of certainty. "That mark upon your arm proves it. You belong to the bell just as much as the rest of us."

Without thinking, Ada's hand went to her forearm, pressing against the bell-shaped mark through her coat sleeve. The gesture did not go unnoticed. Several people in the crowd leaned forward, their eyes fixed upon her arm with a mixture of fear and fascination.

"Show us," Mrs. Fletcher demanded, taking a step closer. Her grief had transformed into something harder, more dangerous. "Show us the mark that saved you while my son dies."

"No," Ada said, backing away. But there was nowhere to go. The crowd pressed in from all sides, their faces twisted with grief and rage and desperate need for someone to blame.

"Show us!" someone shouted from the back of the crowd, and others took up the cry. "Show us the mark!"

Ada felt hands grasping at her coat, pulling at her sleeves. Rough fingers tugged at the wool, trying to expose her arm. She tried to break free, twisting and pulling, but there were too many of them. Their desperation made them strong, their grief made them careless of her fear.

Just as rough fingers found the edge of her sleeve and started to pull it up her arm, a low growl cut through the night air like a blade.

Kito stepped into the circle, his massive form materializing out of the fog like something from a nightmare. His amber eyes reflected the lantern light, seeming to glow with their own inner fire. His lips pulled back to reveal teeth that gleamed white in the darkness, and the thick fur along his spine stood on end. He did not attack, but something in his posture made it clear that he would if anyone took another step toward Ada.

The crowd fell back with gasps and muttered curses, crossing themselves and clutching at protective charms. Some of them had never seen Kito this close before, and his size was intimidating even to those who were accustomed to him. He was no ordinary hyena, and everyone present could sense it.

"Even the beasts protect her," someone whispered, their voice thick with fear and disgust. "Unnatural."

"Witchcraft," muttered another. "That creature is not natural. Nothing that large should move so quietly."

Mrs. Fletcher stared at Kito with wide, frightened eyes, but her grief was stronger than her fear. "Get away from us," she said, her voice breaking. "Take your cursed beast and get away from our grief. You do not belong here."

Ada needed no second telling. She turned and ran, Kito at her side, leaving the angry voices behind. She ran through the fog-choked streets, her feet slipping on the wet cobblestones, past the silent houses with their shuttered windows and barred doors. She could hear them calling after her, their voices carrying accusations and curses through the thick air.

She did not stop running until she reached the rocky shore at the edge of town, where the cobblestones gave way to rough pebbles and weathered stone. The beach was deserted save for the usual debris washed up by the tide. Broken fishing nets tangled with seaweed, pieces of driftwood smooth and gray from years in the salt water, shells ground smooth by countless waves. The fog was thicker here, rolling in from the sea in great gray waves that made the world feel muffled and strange.

Ada collapsed upon a large rock, her chest heaving as she tried to catch her breath. Her lungs burned from the cold air and her desperate flight through the streets. Kito settled beside her, his warm bulk a comfort against the cold night air. She could feel his steady breathing, the solid weight of his presence that had been her only constant companion for years.

She buried her face in her hands and finally let the tears come. They fell hot and fast, mixing with the fog's moisture upon her cheeks. All the anger and grief and helpless frustration of the past seven years poured out of her at once.

They had blamed her again, just as they always did. And perhaps, perhaps they were right. Perhaps her survival had cursed the town to lose more people than it should have. Perhaps every person who had vanished since her night was somehow her fault.

"I'm sorry, Tam," she whispered to the fog, her voice thick with tears. "I am so very sorry."

As if in answer to her words, she heard something impossible. A voice, faint and distant, carried on the wind like the cry of a seabird.

"Ada..."

She lifted her head, wiping her eyes with the back of her hand. The voice came again, clearer this time, unmistakably human.

"Ada... help us..."

Her heart began to race. The voice sounded like Tam, but that was impossible. He was gone, turned to salt and ash like all the others. Unless...

Ada stood slowly, looking out at the fog-shrouded sea. The lighthouse beam cut through the mist, weaker than usual but still pulsing steadily from its perch upon the cliff. And from its direction, she could swear she heard more voices joining Tam's. Whispers and calls, all seeming to know her name.

"Can you hear them as well?" she asked Kito. The hyena's ears were pricked forward, his amber eyes fixed upon the lighthouse. His low rumble of acknowledgment told her that yes, he could hear them too.

The voices were coming from the lighthouse. From whatever lay hidden in its ancient walls. Ada thought of the stories the townspeople told in hushed voices, about a relic called The Channel that could speak to the dead. She had always assumed they were merely stories, folklore meant to frighten children and explain the unexplainable.

But now she was not so certain.

The fog seemed to shift around her, and for a moment, Ada thought she saw shapes moving within it. Faces, perhaps, or hands reaching toward her through the mist. The voices grew stronger, more urgent, overlapping until they became a chorus of whispers all calling her name.

"Find us, Ada. Find The Channel. Before it is too late."

Ada looked back toward town, where the angry voices were still echoing through the streets. She could see the glow of lanterns moving through the fog, people returning to their homes with heavy hearts and empty hands. They would never accept her. They would always blame her for the curse, always see her as a reminder of their losses and their helplessness against forces beyond their control.

But perhaps that didn't matter. Perhaps the real answers were not with the living, who could only offer blame and bitter accusations.

Perhaps they were with the dead.

She pulled her coat tighter around herself and started walking toward the lighthouse, Kito padding silently beside her. The voices grew clearer with each step, and the mark upon her arm began to tingle beneath her sleeve as if responding to their call. Whatever was waiting for her in that crumbling tower, whatever truth lay hidden behind the stories and superstitions, Ada was ready to face it.

Behind her, Lowmere settled into its familiar routine of grief and fear. Ahead, the lighthouse waited upon its cliff, its weak beam calling to her through the fog like a beacon for the lost.

For the first time in seven years, Ada was not running from the curse.

She was walking straight toward it.

Chapter 2:

Whispers in the Night

Ada woke to the sound of voices that shouldn't exist.

She sat up in bed, her heart hammering against her ribs as she strained to listen. The cottage was dark around her, filled with the gray pre-dawn light that never seemed to fully brighten in Lowmere. Outside her window, the fog pressed thick against the glass like curious fingers, and somewhere within its depths, she could hear them.

Whispers. Soft and distant, but unmistakably there.

She had returned from the lighthouse path near midnight, her clothes damp with fog and her mind spinning with questions she couldn't answer. The voices that had called to her from the direction of the old tower had grown fainter as she approached, until she began to doubt she had heard them at all. By the time she reached her cottage, there was only silence and the endless whisper of waves against the rocks below.

But now, hours later, they were back.

Ada slipped from her bed and padded to the window in her bare feet. The floorboards were cold beneath her toes, and she shivered as she pressed her face to the glass. The fog was thicker than she had ever seen it, so dense that she couldn't make out the lighthouse beam that usually cut through the darkness. It was as if the world beyond her cottage had simply ceased to exist.

The whispers grew stronger, and she realized they weren't coming from the lighthouse at all. They were much closer. Right outside her window, in fact, as if whoever was speaking stood just beyond the glass.

"Ada..."

Her breath caught. The voice was soft, almost gentle, but there was something wrong with it. Something that made her skin crawl even as she strained to hear more.

"Ada... help us..."

She pressed her ear to the window, her breath fogging the glass. "Who's there?" she whispered back, feeling foolish even as the words left her lips. But no answer came. There was no one outside. There couldn't be. No one in Lowmere would venture out in fog this thick, especially not to stand outside her cottage and whisper her name.

But the voices continued, layering over each other in a chorus of whispers that made her head spin. She thought she recognized some of them. A voice that might have been Tam Fletcher, though the words were too indistinct to be certain. Another that could have been Sarah Whitmore, who had vanished three years ago. The cadence of old Henrik the fisherman's speech, taken just last spring.

All of them seemed to be speaking her name. All of them seemed to be pleading for something she couldn't understand.

Ada stumbled backward from the window, her hand pressed to her mouth. This couldn't be real. She must be dreaming, or going mad from grief and guilt. Dead people didn't speak to the living. They couldn't.

But even as she tried to convince herself it was all in her mind, she heard something else that made her blood freeze in her veins. A low, rumbling growl from somewhere outside her cottage.

And then a sound she knew all too well. The soft click of claws on stone.

"Kito," she breathed, rushing back to the window. Through the fog, she could just make out a familiar shape moving near her garden gate. The brown hyena stood with his head raised, his amber eyes gleaming faintly in the darkness as he stared at something she couldn't see.

Ada grabbed her coat and boots, pulling them on with shaking hands. If Kito was out there, if he could sense whatever was making these sounds, then something was definitely happening. The hyena had never led her astray before.

She slipped out the back door of her cottage, moving as quietly as she could across the dew-wet grass. The fog enveloped her immediately, so thick she could barely see her own hands. The whispers grew louder as she stepped outside, surrounding her on all sides.

"Ada..."

"Help..."

"Please..."

"Lost..."

The voices overlapped and echoed strangely in the fog, as if they were coming from everywhere and nowhere at once. But when Ada tried to respond, tried to call out "Where are you?" or "What do you need?" the whispers only grew fainter, as if her voice somehow pushed them away.

Ada felt her way along the side of her cottage, using the rough stone wall as a guide until she reached the front garden. Kito stood near the gate, his massive form barely visible in the swirling mist. His fur bristled along his spine, and his lips were pulled back in a silent snarl. But he wasn't looking at Ada. His attention was fixed on something moving in the fog beyond the garden.

"What is it?" Ada whispered, moving to stand beside him.

As if in answer to her question, the fog in front of them began to shift and swirl in patterns that had nothing to do with the wind. Shapes moved within the mist, translucent and barely there, but unmistakably human in form. Ada could make out vague outlines, tall figures, shorter ones, the suggestion of reaching hands and turning faces.

Her heart pounded so hard she thought it might burst from her chest, but she forced herself to stand still. These shapes, whatever they were, seemed connected to the voices she had been hearing.

"Tam?" she called softly to one of the taller figures. "Is that you?"

But the moment she spoke, the shape wavered and began to fade, as if her voice had somehow disrupted whatever force was allowing it to appear. The whispers grew more urgent, more distressed, but remained frustratingly unclear.

"I can't understand you," Ada said desperately. "I can hear you, but I can't make out what you're trying to say. How can I help if I don't know what you need?"

The shapes pressed closer, their forms becoming more agitated. The whispers rose in pitch, overlapping until they became a wall of sound that made Ada's head ache. But still, she couldn't make out individual words or messages. It was as if some barrier existed between her and whatever was trying to communicate, allowing only the faintest impressions to pass through.

Then, as suddenly as they had appeared, the shapes began to fade. The whispers grew quieter, more distant, until they were barely distinguishable from the sound of wind through the grass.

"Wait!" Ada called out. "Don't go! I want to help, but I don't know how!"

But it was too late. The fog was already beginning to thin, and the ghostly figures were gone, dissolved back into the morning mist as if they had never been there at all.

She stood alone in her garden with Kito at her side, the silence pressing down around them like a weight. The fog was still thick, but it no longer carried voices or showed her glimpses of mysterious shapes. It was just fog again, cold and gray and empty.

Ada sank to her knees in the damp grass, her mind reeling from everything she had experienced. The voices of people who sounded like Lowmere's missing, trying desperately to communicate something to her. Shapes in the fog that looked almost human but faded when she tried to interact with them directly.

And the frustrating sense that something important was being lost in translation, that there was a message she needed to hear but couldn't quite grasp.

Kito pressed close to her side, his warm bulk comforting against the morning chill. His amber eyes reflected her own confusion and determination as she looked up at him.

"You saw them too, didn't you?" she asked softly.

The hyena's low rumble of acknowledgment told her everything she needed to know. She wasn't going mad. Something was trying to reach her, something connected to the missing people of her town. But whatever barrier existed between the living and the dead made true communication impossible, at least, not without help.

Ada stood slowly, brushing grass stains from her knees. In the distance, she could hear the sounds of Lowmere waking to another day of grief and fear. Mrs. Fletcher would be weeping over her empty house. Mary Hartwell would be mourning her lost love. The townspeople would gather in small groups to whisper about the curse and cast suspicious glances toward Ada's cottage on the cliff.

But Ada no longer cared what they thought of her. The whispers in the fog had given her purpose, shown her that something beyond the normal world was trying to reach out to her. She had some kind of connection to forces she didn't understand, something that set her apart from the rest of the town.

And she had a feeling that the mysterious lighthouse held answers to questions she was only beginning to form.

The fog began to lift as the sun climbed higher, revealing glimpses of the rocky shore and the ancient tower that stood sentinel on its cliff. The lighthouse looked different in the morning light, less forbidding and more promising. Its weathered stones seemed to call to her, suggesting that within its walls lay the key to understanding what the voices had been trying to tell her.

Ada pulled her coat tighter around herself and started walking toward the lighthouse path, Kito padding silently beside her. Behind them, Lowmere stirred to reluctant life, its people trapped in cycles of grief and superstition that stretched back generations.

But ahead, in the lighthouse on the cliff, lay the possibility of answers. The whispers in the fog had shown her that communication with the missing was possible—she just needed to find the right way to bridge the gap between worlds.

As they walked, Ada felt the mark on her arm tingling, responding to her growing determination. Whatever lay ahead, whatever mysteries waited in the lighthouse, she would face them.

The dead were trying to reach her, and she would not let them down.

Chapter 3:

The Lighthouse

Ada stood at the base of the lighthouse, tilting her head back to look up at its towering height. The ancient stone structure rose from the rocky cliff like a finger pointing toward the gray sky, its walls weathered and cracked from decades of salt spray and storms. Patches of moss clung to the lower stones, and the narrow windows that dotted its sides were dark and empty.

She had passed this lighthouse countless times over the years, but she had never actually ventured inside. Like most people in Lowmere, she had always hurried past it, averting her eyes and quickening her steps. There was something about the tower that made people uneasy, though none could quite say what it was.

But now, after hearing the voices in the fog, after witnessing the trapped spirits of her town's missing people, Ada felt drawn to the lighthouse in a way she never had before. The building seemed to pulse with hidden energy, as if something within was calling to her.

Kito stood beside her, his amber eyes fixed upon the lighthouse door. The heavy wooden barrier was slightly ajar, hanging crooked upon its ancient hinges. Beyond it, Ada could see only darkness.

"Well, then," she said to Kito, trying to keep her voice steady, "I suppose we must venture within."

She reached for the door handle, then paused and turned to the hyena. "Perhaps you should remain out here. I don't know what we will find within, and it might prove dangerous."

Kito's response was immediate and definitive. He pushed past her with surprising gentleness, his massive shoulder nudging her aside as he slipped through the narrow opening. His claws clicked upon the stone floor within, and she heard him snuffling about in the darkness.

"As you will," Ada murmured, following him through the doorway.

The interior of the lighthouse was dim and musty, filled with the smell of salt and old stone. Weak light filtered in through the grimy windows, casting strange shadows across the circular room. The space was larger than Ada had expected, with a spiral staircase winding up along the curved wall toward the beacon chamber far above.

But what caught her attention immediately was how empty the room felt. She had expected to find old furniture, abandoned equipment, perhaps even the belongings of whoever had once tended the lighthouse. Instead, the space was almost bare, as if it had been deliberately cleared out long ago.

Kito was already moving about the room, his nose to the ground as he investigated every corner. His behavior was different here, more alert and focused than usual. His fur seemed to catch the dim light strangely, almost shimmering as he moved.

Ada followed him slowly, running her fingers along the rough stone walls. The surface was carved with deep grooves and strange markings that might have been decorative or might have held deeper meaning. Some of the symbols looked almost familiar, like half-remembered dreams or stories heard in childhood.

"What have you found?" she asked Kito softly.

The hyena had stopped near the base of the spiral staircase, pawing at something upon the floor. Ada knelt beside him and saw that he was scratching at what appeared to be a loose stone. The piece was slightly different from the others around it, newer somehow, as if it had been replaced more recently.

Working together, Ada and Kito managed to pry the stone free. Beneath it lay a small space, just large enough for Ada to reach her hand in. Her fingers touched something smooth and cold, and she carefully withdrew an old iron key.

The key was unlike anything she had ever seen. Its surface was covered with the same strange symbols that decorated the walls, and it seemed to vibrate slightly in her palm, as if it contained some manner of energy.

"What do you suppose this opens?" she asked Kito, but the hyena was already moving toward the staircase, his tail swishing with excitement.

Ada followed him up the winding stairs, the iron steps creaking under their weight. The climb seemed to go on forever, with landing after landing disappearing into the shadows above. Her legs began to ache, and she had to stop several times to catch her breath.

Finally, after what felt like hours but was probably mere minutes, they reached a small landing about halfway up the tower. Here, the staircase continued upward toward the beacon chamber, but there also a door set into the curved wall. It was smaller than the entrance below, made of dark wood that looked far newer than the rest of the lighthouse.

And set into the wood was a keyhole that perfectly matched the iron key in Ada's hand.

"I believe this is what we seek," she said, fitting the key into the lock.

The door opened with surprising ease, swinging inward to reveal a small, circular room. Unlike the empty space below, this chamber was filled with objects. Shelves lined the walls, holding books and scrolls and strange instruments that Ada did not recognize. Candles sat in holders around the room, their wax melted into fantastic shapes but their wicks unburnt.

And in the center of the room, on a round table covered with a dusty cloth, sat something that made Ada's breath catch in her throat.

She stepped closer, Kito pressed against her side, and carefully pulled away the cloth. Beneath it lay a board game unlike anything she had ever seen.

The board was made of dark wood, almost black, and its surface was covered with intricate carvings and symbols. Some of the markings seemed to shift and move in the dim light, though Ada told herself that was only her imagination. Around the edge of the board were letters and numbers, and in the center was a circle divided into sections, each containing a different symbol.

At the top of the board, carved in flowing script, were the words "The Channel."

Beside the board sat other game pieces: A heart-shaped piece of wood with a circular hole in the middle and three small wooden balls for feet, smooth and worn from use. Small tokens made from what appeared to be bone and black stone. Two decks of cards, their backs decorated with the same strange symbols that covered the board itself.

Ada reached out to touch the board, then pulled her hand back. Even from a distance, she could feel energy radiating from it, making her skin tingle and the mark upon her arm pulse with warmth.

"This is it," she whispered to Kito. "This is what the spirits were hinting at. The Channel that can speak to the dead."

Kito moved closer to the table, and Ada gasped. His fur was definitely shimmering now, catching light that seemed not to come from anywhere in the room. His amber eyes glowed brighter than she had ever seen them, reflecting the strange energy that surrounded the game board.

"You can also sense it, can't you?" she said, and Kito's low rumble confirmed her suspicions.

Ada wiped the dust from the board with the corner of the cloth, revealing more of the intricate carvings beneath. The symbols seemed to pulse with faint light as her fingers passed over them, and she could swear she heard whispers at the very edge of her hearing.

She drew out one of the wooden chairs that surrounded the table and sat down carefully. The board was even more beautiful up close, its dark wood polished to a mirror shine despite the dust that had covered it. The craftsmanship was incredible, with every line and curve carved with perfect precision.

But it was also frightening. Ada could feel power radiating from it like heat from a fire, and part of her wished to cover it back up and leave this room forever. This was magic, true magic, and she had no idea what she was venturing into.

Yet the spirits had told her to find The Channel. They had said it would show her the way to end the curse. And if there was even a chance that this strange game could help her save her town, did she not have to try?

Ada took a deep breath and reached for the heart-shaped plank.

The moment her fingers touched the smooth wood, something like lightning shot up her arm. It wasn't painful, exactly, but it was intense, like tiny sparks dancing across her skin. The plank began to glow with soft, pale light, and the symbols around the edge of the board pulsed in response.

Kito became alert and restless, pacing about the small room with his ears pinned back. He kept looking toward the door, as if he expected someone to come through it at any moment.

Ada placed the plank on the board and watched in fascination as it began to move on its own, sliding smoothly across the surface without any guidance from her. It traced patterns among the symbols, pausing at different letters and numbers in what seemed like a deliberate sequence.

"Hello, Ada."

The voice came from everywhere and nowhere, seeming to rise from the board itself. Ada jerked her hands back from the plank, but it continued moving, spelling out words with increasing speed.

"We have been waiting for you."

"Who are you?" Ada whispered, leaning closer to the board.

The plank moved to different letters, spelling out an answer that made her heart race.

"T-H-E L-O-S-T"

More voices joined the first, overlapping and echoing in the small room. Ada recognized some of them. Tam Fletcher, Sarah Whitmore, old Henrik the fisherman. All the people who had vanished on New Moon nights, speaking to her through The Channel.

"You found us," said Tam's voice, warm and grateful. "You found the way to speak with us."

"Where are you?" Ada asked, placing her hands back upon the wooden plank. "The spirits in the fog said you were trapped somewhere."

The plank moved again, and this time the words it spelled made Ada's blood run cold.

"M-O-O-R-L-O-W"

As the name was completed, the room around Ada seemed to shift and blur. The walls became transparent, and beyond them she could see another place entirely. A landscape of twisted trees and rolling fog, where the sky was always twilight and strange lights danced in the distance.

"Moorlow," whispered Sarah's voice. "The Bellringer's realm. We are held here, between life and death, unable to rest."

Ada could see them now, ghostly figures moving through the fog-shrouded landscape. They looked the same as they had in life, but there was a sadness in their faces that made her throat tight with emotion.

"How do I help you?" she asked desperately. "How do I free you from this place?"

But even as she spoke, the vision began to fade. The walls of the lighthouse room solidified around her again, and the voices from The Channel grew fainter.

"The curse must be broken," Tam's voice came to her like an echo from a great distance. "The bargain must be ended. But beware, Ada. The Bellringer knows you have found us now. He will come for you."

"Wait!" Ada called out, pressing her hands more firmly upon the plank. "Don't go! Tell me what I must do!"

But it was too late. The board went silent, its symbols fading back to their normal dark wood appearance. The plank stopped moving and lay still under Ada's hands.

Kito suddenly let out a sharp bark, his hackles rising as he stared at the small window set high in the room's wall. Ada looked up and saw that the sky outside had gone completely black, though it had been midday when they entered the lighthouse.

Lightning cracked across the darkness, illuminating the room in stark white light. Thunder followed immediately, so loud that it seemed to shake the entire lighthouse.

"We must go," Ada said, leaping up from her chair. Something about the sudden storm felt wrong, unnatural. The voices had warned her that the Bellringer would know she had found The Channel, and she had a terrible feeling that the storm was his response.

She seized The Channel board, wrapping it quickly in the dusty cloth. The bone tokens and cards went into her coat pockets, and she tucked the glowing heart-shaped plank safely within her shirt.

Another flash of lightning lit the room, followed immediately by thunder that seemed to come from directly overhead. Rain began to pound against the lighthouse windows, driven by wind that howled like a living thing.

Ada and Kito raced down the spiral staircase, taking the steps two at a time in their haste to escape. Above them, the storm grew stronger, and Ada could swear she heard something else in the wind. A voice, deep and terrible, calling her name with anger that made her bones ache.

They burst out of the lighthouse door and into the driving rain. The storm was worse than anything Ada had ever experienced, with wind so strong it nearly knocked her from her feet and rain that stung like needles against her skin.

But she did not stop running until she reached her cottage, slamming the door behind them and leaning against it as if the storm itself might try to break in. Her clothes were soaked through, and her hair hung in dripping strands around her face.

Kito shook himself, sending water flying across the small living room. His fur had stopped shimmering, but his eyes still held that strange glow, as if the energy from The Channel had left a permanent mark upon him.

Ada unwrapped the board carefully, setting it on her kitchen table where she could examine it more closely. Even here, in the safety of her cottage, she could feel its power. The mark on her arm tingled constantly now, responding to the magical artifact she had brought home.

Outside, the storm continued to rage, but Ada was no longer afraid. She had found The Channel, just as the spirits had told her to. She had spoken with the vanished, seen glimpses of the realm where they were trapped.

And she had taken the first step toward ending the curse that had plagued her town for generations.

Thunder crashed overhead, and Ada smiled grimly as she studied the symbols on the board. Let the Bellringer rage. Let him send all the storms he wished.

She had work to do.

Chapter 4:

Secrets of Moorlow

The storm raged outside Ada's cottage for three days.

She had never seen weather such as this. The wind howled with voices that seemed almost human, and the rain hammered against her windows with such force that she feared the glass might shatter. Lightning split the sky in jagged patterns that pained the eyes to behold, and thunder shook her cottage until the dishes rattled in her cupboards.

But Ada barely noticed the storm. She was too absorbed in The Channel.

She had set up the board on her kitchen table immediately after returning from the lighthouse, and she had hardly moved from that spot since. The bone tokens clicked softly under her fingers as she arranged and rearranged them according to patterns that felt familiar even though she had never seen them before. The cards lay spread around the board's edge, their strange symbols seeming to shift and change when she was not looking directly at them.

And the plank. The heart-shaped piece of wood had become warm in her hands, pulsing with gentle energy that made the mark upon her arm tingle in response. Every time she placed it upon the board, voices filled her cottage. The voices of Lowmere's missing, speaking to her from whatever dark realm held them prisoner.

Kito had not left her side during the three days of the storm. The brown hyena lay curled near her chair, his amber eyes reflecting the strange light that emanated from The Channel whenever Ada used it. His fur still held that odd shimmer it had gained in the lighthouse, and sometimes Ada caught him staring at the board with an expression that seemed almost human in its intensity.

On the third night, as thunder crashed overhead and lightning painted her cottage walls in stark white light, Ada placed her hands upon the plank once more.

"Are you there?" she asked softly.

The response was immediate. The plank began to move smoothly across the board, guided by invisible hands, spelling out words with practiced ease.

"W-E A-R-E H-E-R-E"

More voices joined the first, layering over each other in a chorus that filled the small cottage. Ada had learned to distinguish between them over the past few days. Tam Fletcher's voice was warm and gentle, always encouraging. Sarah Whitmore spoke with urgency, as if time was running short. Old Henrik had a gravelly tone that reminded her of waves grinding against pebbles.

"We have been waiting," said Tam's voice, warm with affection. "Waiting for you to return to us."

"Tell me more about the curse," Ada said, leaning closer to the board. "You said it was connected to the founding families. What did you mean by this?"

The plank moved more quickly now, spelling out words faster than Ada could follow. But she did not need to read them. The voices spoke directly to her, painting pictures in her mind with their words.

"Long ago," began Sarah's voice, "when Lowmere was naught but a handful of fishing huts upon a dangerous coast, the sea was our enemy. Ships were lost every season. Fishermen who went out in the morning never returned by night. The waves claimed so many lives that the survivors began to speak of leaving, of finding some safer place to build their homes."

Ada could see it in her mind as Sarah spoke. A younger Lowmere, smaller and more fragile, perched upon cliffs that offered little protection from the hungry sea. She could almost hear the crash of waves against stone, the cries of families watching their loved ones sail into storms that would swallow them whole.

"The founding families were desperate," continued Henrik's gruff voice. "The Thornes, the Blackwoods, the Merrows, and the Grays. Four families who had led their people to this cursed coast and felt responsible for every life the sea claimed."

Ada's breath caught. "Thorne? Did you speak the name Thorne?"

"Aye," said Tam gently. "Your family, Ada. The Thornes were one of the founding families, and their blood runs in your veins."

The mark upon Ada's arm began to pulse with warmth, as if responding to the name. She pressed her free hand against it, feeling the raised outline of the bell through her shirt sleeve.

"What happened to them?" she asked. "What did they do?"

The voices grew quieter, more serious, as if the tale they were about to tell was almost too terrible to speak aloud.

"They made a bargain," whispered Sarah. "In their desperation, they called out to powers beyond the mortal world. They begged the sea to spare their people, to grant them safe passage and calm waters."

"And the sea answered," added Henrik grimly. "But not in the manner they had hoped."

Ada could see it happening as the voices painted the scene for her. The four founding families, standing upon the cliff where her cottage now sat, their faces drawn with grief and desperation. The fog rolling in from the ocean, thicker than any natural mist. And emerging from that fog, a figure that belonged neither to the world of the living nor the realm of the dead.

"Malrik," breathed Tam's voice. "The Bellringer. A creature caught between worlds, neither man nor spirit, with power over the boundaries between life and death."

"He offered them a bargain," continued Sarah. "Calm seas in exchange for tribute. One life every New Moon, claimed by the toll of his bell. The founding families were horrified, but the alternative was watching their entire community die one shipwreck at a time."

Ada felt sick. She could imagine the impossible choice those long-dead ancestors had faced. Save everyone by sacrificing a few, or lose everyone to the hungry sea.

"They agreed," she said, though it was not a question.

"They agreed," confirmed Henrik sadly. "They bound their bloodlines to the bargain, sealing it with their own magic. The curse would claim one soul every New Moon until the debt was paid in full."

"But what debt?" Ada asked, confusion and anger rising in her voice. "How many lives would be enough? When would it end?"

The silence that followed was heavier than the storm outside. When the voices finally spoke again, there was a weight to their words that made Ada's heart sink.

"The debt has no end," said Sarah quietly. "The bargain was made in desperation, without thought for the future. Malrik's hunger grows with each soul claimed, and the price increases with each generation. What began as one life per New Moon has become something far more dangerous."

"The curse is changing," added Tam, his voice filled with worry. "We can feel it from within Moorlow, the shadow realm where we are held. The Bellringer grows stronger, and his appetite grows larger. Soon, he shall not be content with one soul per month. He will take more and more until Lowmere is naught but an empty shell."

Ada's hands trembled upon the plank. "How long do we have?"

"Not long," whispered Henrik. "Perhaps a year, perhaps less. The curse feeds upon itself now, growing stronger with each life claimed. And your survival seven years ago has made it hungrier still."

The words struck Ada like a physical blow. She had hoped that the spirits would tell her she bore no responsibility for the increased frequency of disappearances, but instead, they were confirming her worst fears.

"I made it worse," she said, her voice breaking. "By surviving when I should have died, I made the curse stronger."

"Nay," said Tam firmly, his voice cutting through her despair. "You did not choose to survive, Ada. Your bloodline protected you, just as it was meant to."

"What do you mean?"

The plank began moving again, spelling out words that made Ada's heart race with possibility.

"T-H-E F-O-U-N-D-I-N-G F-A-M-I-L-I-E-S K-N-E-W"

"Knew what?" Ada asked breathlessly.

"They knew the bargain could not last forever," explained Sarah. "When they bound their bloodlines to the curse, they also wove into it a way out. A method by which their descendant could break the bargain and free the town from Malrik's power."

Ada felt her pulse quicken. "How? What did they do?"

"They left a legacy," said Henrik. "A birthright that would pass down through the generations until it reached someone with the strength and will to face the Bellringer in his own realm. Someone who could walk between worlds and challenge the curse at its source."

The mark upon Ada's arm was burning now, pulsing with heat that spread through her entire body. She pulled up her sleeve and gasped at what she saw. The bell-shaped outline was glowing with soft, pale light, its edges more defined than they had ever been before.

"The mark," she breathed.

"The mark of the chosen," confirmed Tam gently. "It appeared when you survived the bell's call because you are the one the founding families prepared for. The last hope of breaking the curse they created."

Ada stared at the glowing symbol on her arm, trying to process what the spirits were telling her. She was not merely a random survivor of the curse. She was part of it, bred for it, chosen by her own ancestors to be its destroyer.

"I do not understand," she said, her voice small and lost. "If I am supposed to break the curse, why do I not know how? Why was I not told of any of this?"

"Because the knowledge was hidden," said Sarah sadly. "After the bargain was made, the founding families realized what they had done. The guilt and horror of their choice drove them to madness. They scattered the clues, buried the truth, hoping that future generations would be spared the burden of their sins."

"But the magic remained," added Henrik. "Dormant in the bloodlines, waiting for the right moment to awaken. Your survival triggered it, Ada. The mark upon your arm is proof that you carry the power to end what your ancestors began."

Ada looked around her cottage, at the storm raging outside, at Kito watching her with those strangely glowing eyes. Everything felt different now. The weight of centuries pressed down upon her shoulders, and she could feel the expectations of the dead surrounding her like a physical presence.

"What if I'm not strong enough?" she whispered. "What if I fail?"

"Then Lowmere dies," said Tam simply. "And we remain trapped in Moorlow forever, watching as the Bellringer spreads his curse to other towns, other coasts. The hunger shall not stop with your home, Ada. It will grow until it consumes everything in its path."

The words sent ice through her veins. She had thought the curse would be limited to Lowmere, contained by the original bargain. But if it could spread, if other communities could fall victim to Malrik's hunger, then the stakes were higher than she had ever imagined.

"Tell me what I must do," she said, her voice gaining strength. "Tell me how to break the curse."

But even as she spoke, she could feel the connection growing weaker. The storm outside was reaching a crescendo, and the voices from The Channel were fading like echoes in a vast chamber.

"The knowledge is scattered," came Tam's voice, barely audible now. "Hidden in places of power throughout Lowmere. You must find the pieces and put them together."

"Where?" Ada asked desperately. "Where must I look?"

"The old places," whispered Sarah. "Where the founding families lived and worked and hid their secrets. The lighthouse was merely the beginning, Ada. There is much more to find."

"And beware," added Henrik, his voice like wind through dead leaves. "The Bellringer knows you have The Channel now. He will try to stop you, to claim you before you can challenge his power. Trust none save those who have already paid the price."

The voices faded to nothing, leaving Ada alone in her cottage with only the sound of the storm for company. The heart-shaped plank lay still under her hands, its wood warm but silent. The symbols upon the board had returned to their normal dark appearance, as if the conversation had never happened.

But the mark upon her arm still glowed with soft light, proof that everything she had heard was real.

Ada sat back in her chair, her mind reeling with everything she had learned. She was a descendant of Lowmere's founding families, chosen by her ancestors to break a curse they had created in desperation. The bell-shaped mark upon her arm was not a reminder of her survival but a sign of her destiny. And somewhere in Lowmere, hidden in the old places where her family had once lived and worked, were the clues she needed to fulfill that destiny.

Kito rose from his spot by her chair and padded to the window, his ears pricked forward. The storm was finally beginning to weaken, the thunder growing more distant and the rain subsiding to a steady patter. But Ada knew this was only the calm before a greater storm.

The Bellringer knew she had The Channel now. He would come for her, just as the spirits had warned. And when he did, she would need to be ready.

She looked down at the board upon her table, at the tokens and cards that held so much power and mystery. The spirits had told her the knowledge was scattered, hidden in the old places of Lowmere. On the morrow, when the storm ended, she would begin her search.

But tonight, she would prepare. She would study The Channel more closely, learn its secrets, try to understand the magic that flowed through her bloodline. The mark upon her arm pulsed with warmth, as if responding to her determination.

Outside, the storm began to die away, but Ada barely noticed. She had work to do, and not much time in which to do it. The curse was growing stronger, and according to the spirits, she had perhaps a year before it consumed everything she cared about.

But she was no longer merely Ada the outcast, the girl marked by survival and blamed for tragedies beyond her control. She was Ada Thorne, descendant of the founding families, chosen by fate and blood to face an ancient evil.

And she would not let her ancestors' sacrifice be in vain.

Thunder rumbled in the distance as Ada reached for the wooden plank once more. There was still so much to learn, so much to understand. But for the first time since the thirteenth bell had tolled for her seven years ago, she felt something other than fear and guilt.

She felt purpose.

The storm was ending, but Ada's true journey was just beginning.

Chapter 5:

Trust and Truths

The morning after the storm had ended, Ada woke to find Lowmere much changed.

She stood at her kitchen window, gazing out over the town that had been her home these fourteen years, and scarcely recognized it. The three-day tempest had left its mark upon all things. Trees lay uprooted across the cobblestone streets, their massive trunks barring pathways that had been clear for generations. Roof tiles littered the ground like scattered leaves, and several of the older houses leaned at angles that suggested their foundations had been damaged beyond all repair.

But it was not merely the physical destruction that made Lowmere seem different. There was something else in the air—a tension that made Ada's skin crawl and the mark on her arm tingle with constant warmth. The fog that perpetually shrouded the town had taken on a strange quality, swirling in patterns that seemed almost purposeful. And in the distance, she could see people moving through the streets with an urgency that spoke of fresh fear.

Kito appeared at her side, pressing his warm bulk against her legs. The hyena's amber eyes were fixed upon the town below, and his ears were pinned back against his skull. Whatever he sensed out there did not bode well.

"Something is amiss, is it not?" Ada asked softly, running her fingers through his coarse fur. "More amiss than is usual, I mean to say."

Kito's low rumble of agreement sent a shiver down her spine. The storm had not been natural, and its effects lingered in ways that had nothing to do with fallen trees and broken roof tiles.

Ada turned away from the window and seated herself at her kitchen table, where The Channel awaited her. Over the past three days, the board had become the center of her world. She had learned to read its symbols more clearly, to understand the subtle differences between the various spirits who spoke through it. But more than that, she had begun to feel a connection to the trapped souls that went beyond mere communication.

They trusted her now in a way that the living never had. When she placed her hands upon the heart-shaped plank, their voices welcomed her like an old friend returning home. They shared their memories with her, their pain and their hopes, painting pictures of a Lowmere she had never known.

"Are you there?" she asked, settling her fingers upon the heart-shaped wooden piece.

The response was immediate and warm, like stepping into sunlight after a long winter.

"Always," came Tam Fletcher's voice, filled with affection. "We are always here for you, Ada."

Other voices joined his, creating the familiar chorus that had become her daily companion. But today there seemed to be more of them, as if the storm had somehow strengthened the connection between worlds.

"You appear weary," said Sarah Whitmore, her tone gentle with concern. "The storm kept you from rest, did it not?"

Ada nodded, though she knew the spirits could not see the gesture. "It was not a natural storm, was it? It was him—the Bellringer."

"Aye," confirmed old Henrik, his gruff voice heavy with worry. "Malrik knows you possess The Channel now. The storm was his manner of testing your resolve, of trying to frighten you into abandoning your search for the truth."

"Did it succeed?" asked a new voice, one Ada did not recognize. It was a woman's voice, cultured and strong, with an accent that seemed older than the others.

"No," Ada said firmly. "It did not. If anything, it made me more determined."

"Good," said the unknown woman, and Ada could hear approval in her tone. "Then you truly are a daughter of the Thorne line. We do not frighten with ease."

Ada's breath caught. "We? Are you...?"

"I am Elara Thorne," the voice said, and suddenly Ada could feel a presence stronger than any of the others, as if this spirit stood closer to the boundary between worlds. "Your fifth foremother, child. I was the last of our line to know the full truth about the curse before the knowledge was scattered and hidden."

Ada's hands trembled upon the plank. To speak with an ancestor, someone who shared her blood and her burden, felt like coming home after a lifetime of wandering.

"You knew?" she asked. "You knew what I was meant to do?"

"I helped prepare the way for you, yes," Elara said, her voice filled with ancient sadness. "Though I prayed you would

49

never need to walk this path. The weight of what our family did, the lives we sacrificed for the sake of the many, has haunted every generation since the bargain was made."

The plank began to move more swiftly, spelling out words that painted pictures in Ada's mind. She could see Elara Thorne as clearly as if she stood in the room. A tall woman with dark hair and eyes that were the same heterochromatic mix of brown and green Ada possessed. She wore the garb of a previous generation, but her face held the same determination that Ada saw in her own reflection.

"Tell me of them," Ada said softly. "Tell me of the others who tried to break the curse."

The silence that followed was heavy with grief, and when the spirits spoke again, their voices were thick with remembered pain.

"There have been three before you," Elara said slowly. "Three descendants of the founding families who carried the mark and tried to challenge Malrik's power."

"The first was my younger brother, Marcus," she continued, and Ada could hear the heartbreak in her voice even across the span of death. "He was brave and strong, and he believed that his will alone would be enough to break the bargain. He entered Moorlow through The Channel, just as you must, but he was not prepared for what he found there."

Ada felt ice forming in her stomach. "What became of him?"

"Malrik claimed him," Henrik said quietly. "Turned him into another voice in the chorus of the lost. His strength became the Bellringer's strength, and the curse grew hungrier because of it."

"The second was my own daughter, Evangeline," Elara continued, her voice breaking with ancient grief. "She was wiser than Marcus, more careful in her preparations. She studied the old texts, gathered allies, prepared for months before making her attempt. But knowledge alone was not sufficient."

"She tried to bargain with Malrik," added Sarah sadly. "Tried to negotiate new terms for the curse. But you cannot reason with a creature that exists only to consume. Her compassion became her downfall."

Ada's mark pulsed with heat, and she pressed her free hand against it. "And the third?"

"My grandson, your third forefather Thomas," Elara said. "He was the cleverest of us all, and perhaps the most desperate. The curse had taken his wife, his children, all whom he loved. He went into Moorlow not to break the bargain but to destroy it entirely, to burn away the magic that bound our families to Malrik's hunger."

The plank moved frantically across the board, and Ada could feel the urgency in her ancestor's words.

"He came closer than any before him," Elara said. "He found the heart of Malrik's power, the source of the Bellringer's strength. But at the crucial moment, his rage betrayed him. Instead of surgical precision, he brought wild fury, and the backlash nearly destroyed both worlds."

"What do you mean?" Ada asked, though part of her already dreaded the answer.

"The curse did not merely grow stronger," Tam explained. "It changed. What had been a steady, predictable toll became something more erratic, more hungry. The bells began to ring more often, and the souls they claimed were no longer just from Lowmere."

Ada felt sick. "Other towns?"

"Small villages along the coast," Henrik confirmed. "Fishing communities that had no connection to the original bargain. Thomas's attempt to destroy the curse had freed it from some of its original constraints, allowed it to spread beyond the boundaries set by the founding families."

"That is why the knowledge was scattered after his death," Elara said. "That is why each generation has known less than the one before. The surviving families were terrified that another attempt might make things even worse."

Ada sat back in her chair, overwhelmed by the weight of failure that surrounded her legacy. Three attempts to break the curse, three descendants who had tried and died, and each failure had made the situation more desperate.

"But how am I supposed to succeed where they failed?" she asked, her voice small and lost. "If Marcus's strength was not enough, if Evangeline's wisdom was not enough, if Thomas's desperation was not enough, what makes you think I can do any better?"

The silence stretched out for long moments, and Ada began to fear that the spirits had abandoned her. But when Elara's voice came again, it was filled with something that had not been there before: hope.

"Because you have something they did not," her ancestor said gently. "You have The Channel."

"But Thomas had it as well," Ada protested. "You said he was your grandson, so he must have been able to use it."

"He had access to it, aye," Elara confirmed. "But The Channel was incomplete then. Broken. The storm that brought Malrik to our shores also shattered the original artifact, and we only managed to recover fragments of it. Each generation since has been slowly rebuilding it, piece by piece, adding to its power."

Ada looked down at the board on her table, its dark wood gleaming in the morning light. "This is the complete version?"

"As complete as it can be in this world," said Sarah. "But there is more to it than just the board and pieces you see. The Channel exists in both worlds simultaneously, and in Moorlow it has powers that cannot be accessed from the realm of the living."

"What kind of powers?" Ada asked.

"The power to bind as well as communicate," explained Henrik. "The power to command as well as request. In Moorlow, The Channel is not just a tool for speaking with the dead but a weapon capable of challenging the Bellringer upon equal terms."

Ada felt a flutter of something that might have been hope. "So I have advantages they did not?"

"Aye," Elara said firmly. "But you also face dangers they never encountered. With each failed attempt, Malrik has grown stronger, more cunning. He knows the patterns now, the ways our family thinks and acts. He shall be ready for you in ways he was not ready for them."

The weight of expectation settled upon Ada's shoulders like a lead cloak. Not only was she carrying the hopes of the dead, but she was facing an enemy who had learned from decades of victory. An enemy who knew her weaknesses before she even discovered them herself.

"I am afraid," she admitted quietly. "I am afraid I will fail as they did and make everything worse."

"Fear is not weakness," Elara said gently. "Fear is wisdom. Marcus went into Moorlow without fear, and it made him reckless. Evangeline went with too much fear, and it made her hesitate at crucial moments. Thomas went with naught but rage, and it blinded him to the consequences of his actions."

"Then what should I feel?" Ada asked.

"Balance," came the answer from multiple voices at once. "Courage tempered by caution. Determination guided by wisdom. Strength softened by compassion."

"But most importantly," added Elara, "you must understand that this is not a burden you carry alone. The previous attempts failed because each of them tried to face Malrik in isolation, cutting themselves off from help in their pride or desperation."

Ada looked around her cottage, at Kito lying by her feet, at the empty chairs and silent rooms that had been her only companions for years. "But I am alone. The townspeople hate me, blame me for the curse. Who could possibly aid me?"

"We," said Tam simply. "The souls trapped in Moorlow. We have been gathering strength for years, preparing for another attempt. This time, you shall not face the Bellringer alone."

"And there are others," Sarah added. "Living souls in Lowmere who know more than they pretend, who have been waiting for a sign that the time has come to act."

Ada felt a spark of curiosity pierce through her fear. "Who? Who else knows the truth?"

"You shall find them when you are ready," Elara said mysteriously. "When you have proven yourself capable of carrying the burden. But first, you must learn more about what you face. You must understand not just the history of the curse but its current state, its weaknesses, its plans for the future."

The plank began to move more urgently, and Ada sensed that their time was running short. The connection between worlds was never stable for long, and longer conversations required more energy than the spirits could maintain indefinitely.

"The curse is changing," Henrik said swiftly. "Evolving. What began as a simple exchange of souls has become something far more complex. Malrik is no longer content to simply claim lives. He is building something in Moorlow, gathering power for a purpose we do not fully understand."

"What sort of something?" Ada asked, but the voices were already growing fainter.

"An anchor," came Elara's voice, barely audible. "A way to merge the worlds, to bring Moorlow into the realm of the living. If he succeeds, the curse shall no longer be limited to New Moon nights. It shall be constant, consuming everything in its path."

The plank went still beneath Ada's hands, and silence filled the cottage. The spirits had used all their strength to maintain such a long conversation, and it would be hours before she could contact them again.

But Ada did not need to hear more to understand the magnitude of what she faced. The curse was not merely threatening Lowmere anymore. If Malrik succeeded in his plans, if he found a way to merge the worlds, then every living thing upon the coast would be in danger.

She rose from the table and walked to her window, gazing out over the storm-damaged town. In the distance, she could see people moving through the streets, beginning the long process of cleaning up and rebuilding. They had no notion that their efforts might be meaningless, that they faced a threat far greater than fallen trees and broken roof tiles.

But Ada knew. And knowledge brought responsibility.

She turned back to The Channel, studying its symbols with new understanding. This was more than merely a tool for speaking with the dead. It was a weapon, forged by her ancestors and perfected over generations, designed specifically to challenge the creature they had foolishly invited into their world.

Kito rose from his spot by her feet and came to stand beside her, his amber eyes reflecting the morning light. The shimmer in his fur had grown more pronounced over the past few days, and Ada wondered if he, too, was changing, adapting to the magic that surrounded them.

"We have work to do," she told him quietly. "Elara said there were others who knew the truth, people who could aid us. We must find them."

But even as she spoke, Ada felt the weight of isolation pressing down upon her. The townspeople blamed her for the curse, treated her like a disease to be avoided. How could she possibly convince any of them to help her, especially when doing so would put them in mortal danger?

The answer came to her gradually, like dawn breaking over the horizon. She could not convince them with words. But she could convince them with actions. By proving that she was more than merely a survivor, more than merely a reminder of their losses.

By showing them that she was their salvation.

Ada wrapped The Channel carefully in its cloth and tucked it away in the old chest where her mother had once kept her most precious belongings. The board would be safe there until she needed it again, protected by wards her ancestor had woven into the very stones of the cottage.

Outside, Lowmere was beginning another day in the shadow of the curse. People would go about their daily routines, pretending that normalcy was still possible, that the thirteenth bell was not counting down to their doom with every passing New Moon.

But Ada knew better now. She knew the truth about her heritage, about her destiny, about the impossible task that lay ahead of her. And for the first time since the mark had appeared upon her arm seven years past, she felt ready to embrace it.

The spirits had given her more than merely knowledge. They had given her purpose, and purpose was something she had been lacking for far too long.

She pulled on her coat and headed for the door, Kito at her side. It was time to cease hiding from the townspeople who blamed her, time to cease accepting their judgment without question.

It was time to begin her true work.

The curse might be growing stronger, and Malrik might be preparing to merge the worlds, but Ada was no longer merely a frightened girl marked by survival. She was the last hope of the founding families, trained by the dead and armed with their accumulated wisdom.

And she would not disappoint them.

Chapter 6:

Echoes of the Past

Ada returned to the lighthouse at dawn, when the fog was thickest and the streets of Lowmere were yet empty. She had spent the night pondering what Elara had told her, about the knowledge that had been scattered and hidden throughout the town. If she were to find the pieces she needed to complete her understanding of the curse, she would have to start where her family's involvement had begun.

The lighthouse stood silent upon its cliff, its weathered stones dark with moisture from the morning mist. But as Ada approached the ancient structure, she noticed things she had missed during her first visit. Carved into the stone blocks near the entrance were symbols that appeared familiar, echoes of the markings she had seen upon The Channel's surface.

Kito padded beside her, his amber eyes alert and focused. The hyena seemed different this morning, more purposeful somehow, as if he knew they were upon the verge of discovering something of import. His fur caught the weak morning light strangely, that otherworldly shimmer more pronounced than ever.

"Let us see what else this place has to show us," Ada murmured, pushing open the heavy wooden door.

Within the lighthouse, the circular room appeared different in the daylight filtering through the grimy windows. Ada could see details that had been hidden in shadow the last time she'd been there. The walls were covered with more carvings than she had initially noticed, symbols and markings that seemed to tell a story if only she could read them properly.

But it was Kito who found the first true clue.

The hyena had gone straight to the far wall, where he stood sniffing at what appeared to be ordinary stone blocks. But as Ada knelt beside him, she could see that one section of the wall was different from the rest. The stones were slightly newer, and the mortar between them had a different color and texture.

Working together, they managed to pry loose several of the stones, revealing a small hidden compartment behind them. Within, wrapped in oiled leather that had protected them from decades of moisture, were several items that made Ada's heart race with excitement.

The first was a collection of letters tied with a faded ribbon. The paper was yellowed with age, but the ink was still clearly legible. At the top of the first letter, written in an elegant script, was a name that made Ada's breath catch: Elara Thorne.

The second item was a small leather-bound book, its cover worn smooth by countless hands. When Ada opened it carefully, she found page after page of handwritten entries in the same script as the letters. A journal, kept by her great-great-great grandmother during the years leading up to her death.

But it was the third item that made Kito suddenly alert and restless. It was a small carved figure, no larger than Ada's palm, depicting a hyena in remarkable detail. The carving was old, much older than the letters or journal, and it radiated the same strange energy she had come to associate with magical objects.

"Is that...?" Ada began, looking from the carving to Kito.

The hyena's low rumble seemed almost like laughter, and for a moment, his amber eyes held an intelligence that was startlingly human.

Ada tucked the items carefully into her coat and headed for the lighthouse's spiral staircase. But instead of ascending to the room where she had found The Channel, she descended to a level she had not explored before. Below the main chamber was a basement carved directly into the cliff stone, and it was here that she found what she sought.

The walls of the basement were covered with more carvings, but these were different from the ones above. They were older, more primitive, and they told a story in pictures that made Ada's skin crawl with recognition. She could see the four founding families standing upon the cliff, their faces raised to the storm-tossed sky. She could see the fog rolling in from the sea, and emerging from it, a tall figure with eyes that seemed to burn even in stone.

Scattered throughout the carvings were images of hyenas, always standing beside the human figures, always watching with those intelligent eyes.

"You have been here all along, haven't you?" Ada asked Kito softly. "Not merely with me, but with my family for generations."

Kito pressed close to her side, his warmth comforting in the cold basement air. When Ada looked down at him, she could swear she saw him nod.

Ada spent another hour exploring the lighthouse basement, but she found nothing else that seemed immediately useful. The carvings told the story she already knew, and while seeing it depicted in stone made it feel more real, it did not provide the practical knowledge she needed.

As they climbed back up to the main level, Ada opened one of Elara's letters and began to read by the gray light from the windows. The elegant script was faded but legible, and the words painted a picture of a woman struggling with an impossible burden.

My dearest Thomas, I fear I may not live to see you grown, so I write these words in hopes that they shall reach you when you have need of them most. The curse that plagues our family grows stronger with each generation, and I sense that the time approaches when one of our blood must make the final choice.

Ada's hands trembled as she continued reading. The letter was dated nearly one hundred years earlier, written by Elara to Thomas, Ada's great-grandfather.

The knowledge our ancestors hid is scattered throughout Lowmere, hidden in places that hold meaning for our family. I have found some of the pieces, but not all. Look for the old Thorne house upon Millfield Lane, where your third forefather once dwelt. Look for the workshop behind the Blackwood Inn, where the original Channel was first assembled. Look for the memorial stones in the old cemetery, where truths are carved in plain sight but written in codes only our bloodline can decipher.

Ada's pulse quickened. Elara was giving her a map, a guide to finding the scattered knowledge she needed. But the letter continued with warnings that made her stomach clench with fear.

But be careful, my dear boy. The Bellringer watches always, and he grows more cunning with each passing year. He knows our family's patterns, our ways of thinking and acting. Trust no one completely, save the guardian who has protected our line since the beginning. The hyena carries more wisdom than any human, and his loyalty spans centuries.

Ada looked up from the letter to find Kito watching her with those unnaturally intelligent eyes. "The guardian," she whispered. "That is what you are, isn't it? You have been protecting my family for generations."

This time, there was no mistaking it. Kito definitely nodded, a distinctly human gesture that should have been impossible for an animal to make.

Ada folded the letter carefully and tucked it back into her coat with the others. She had what she came for, and now she needed to follow Elara's directions to the next piece of the puzzle.

The old Thorne house upon Millfield Lane.

Ada had never heard of Millfield Lane, but she had a feeling she would recognize it when she found it. The Thorne family name was not common in Lowmere, and she had always assumed her parents were the last of the line. To learn that there had been others, that there was a house somewhere in town that had once belonged to her relatives, filled her with a mixture of excitement and dread.

She and Kito left the lighthouse and made their way back toward the town center. The fog was beginning to lift slightly, revealing more of the damage caused by the storm than Ada had seen from her cottage window. Entire sections of roofs had been torn away, and several buildings leaned at precarious angles. The people she saw moving through the streets appeared haggard and frightened, speaking in hushed voices and glancing nervously at the sky.

But Ada scarcely noticed their fear. She was too focused upon finding Millfield Lane, following a mental map drawn from fragments of family history and half-remembered stories.

She found it at last, tucked away in the oldest part of town where the streets curved and twisted like the paths of some ancient maze. Millfield Lane was scarcely more than an alley, so narrow that two people could barely walk side by side. The buildings that lined it were older than anything else in Lowmere, their stone foundations dating back to the town's earliest days.

At the end of the lane, nearly hidden behind a tangle of overgrown vines and neglected trees, stood a house that made Ada's heart skip a beat.

It was small and modest, built from the same dark stone as the lighthouse, but there was something about its proportions and design that felt immediately familiar. As if she had seen it before in dreams or in memories that were not quite her own.

The windows were boarded up, and the front door was secured with a heavy chain and padlock. But when Ada approached the barrier, she noticed that the lock was old and corroded, weakened by years of salt air and neglect.

"Keep watch," she told Kito, who positioned himself at the mouth of the alley like a sentinel.

Ada found a loose cobblestone and used it to break the weakened lock. The chain fell away with a rusty clatter, and the front door swung open upon hinges that screeched in protest.

The interior of the house was dark and thick with dust, but shafts of light filtering through gaps in the boarded windows provided just enough illumination for Ada to see. The rooms were small and cramped by modern standards, but they had been furnished with obvious care and attention to detail. Furniture sat beneath cloth covers that had once been white but were now gray with age and neglect.

But it was the walls that captured Ada's attention. Every surface was covered with paintings, drawings, and written notes that seemed to chronicle decades of research into the curse. Maps of Lowmere marked with strange symbols, genealogical charts tracing the bloodlines of the founding families, and page after page of handwritten observations about the pattern of disappearances.

In the center of the main room stood a desk that had obviously been the heart of whoever's research this had been. The surface was covered with papers and books, all arranged as if the occupant had simply stepped out for a moment and was due to return at any time.

Ada approached the desk carefully, her footsteps echoing in the empty house. The papers were covered with the same elegant handwriting she had seen in Elara's letters, but these notes were more recent. Some were dated only twenty years ago, which meant they had been written long after Elara's death.

The pattern accelerates, one note read. *Three disappearances this year instead of the usual one per month. The curse grows hungrier, and I fear we are running out of time.*

Another note, written in a different hand, responded: *The bloodline grows thin. Only one child remains of the main Thorne branch, and she is too young to understand her destiny. We must preserve the knowledge for her, hide it where she shall find it when the time comes.*

Ada's hands shook as she realized what she was reading. These were communications between different members of her family, people who had known about the curse and her role in ending it. People who had been preparing for her arrival long before she was even born.

She searched through the papers more systematically, looking for anything that might provide practical guidance. Most of the notes dealt with historical research or observations about the curse's behavior, but at last she found what she sought.

Hidden beneath a stack of genealogical charts was a journal bound in black leather. Unlike Elara's elegant script, this journal was written in a hasty, urgent hand that suggested its author had been working under pressure.

The Channel is only part of the key, the first entry read. *Elara's research was correct, but incomplete. To challenge Malrik in his own realm, the descendant must carry items of power from each of the founding families. The Thorne line provides the blood and the mark. The Blackwoods provided the wood from which The Channel was carved. The Merrows contributed the bone tokens that focus its energy. And the Grays...*

The entry cut off there, as if the author had been interrupted. But Ada found the continuation several pages later.

The Grays were the most secretive of the founding families, and their contribution to the original bargain was kept hidden even from the others. But I have found references to artifacts they created, items of protection that could shield the bearer from Malrik's most dangerous attacks. If these items yet exist, they would be hidden in the Gray family vault beneath the old cemetery.

Ada's heart raced as she read on. The journal was a treasure trove of practical information, detailing not merely the history of the curse but specific steps that could be taken to combat it. The author had clearly spent years researching and planning for the moment when a Thorne descendant would finally make the attempt to break the bargain.

But it was the final entry that made Ada's blood run cold.

I can feel him watching me now. Malrik knows what I have discovered, and he shall not allow me to share it. I can only hope that these notes shall survive long enough to reach the one they were meant for. To my descendant who reads this: The battle you face is not merely for Lowmere but for the entire world. If Malrik succeeds in merging the realms, his hunger shall spread across the earth like a plague. You are the last hope of stopping him, but you need not face him alone. Trust the guardian, trust the spirits, and trust the magic that flows in your blood. The founding families' greatest sin may also be their greatest gift.

The journal was signed with a name that made Ada's throat tight with emotion: *Your second forefather, Jonathan Thorne.*

She had never known her grandfather, had been told he died before she was born. But here was proof that he had lived long enough to research the curse, to understand her destiny, and to prepare the way for her arrival. He had died protecting the knowledge she needed, and his sacrifice had made her current quest possible.

Ada carefully gathered up the most important papers and notes from the desk, rolling them up and tucking them inside her coat alongside Elara's letters. She also took several small objects that her grandfather's journal had marked as potentially useful: a silver pendant carved with protective symbols, a small knife with a bone handle, and a pouch of what appeared to be ordinary salt but had been blessed according to rituals described in the journal.

As she prepared to leave the abandoned house, Ada took one last look around the rooms where her grandfather had spent his final years. The walls seemed to whisper with the echoes of his research, with the weight of knowledge accumulated and preserved through generations of sacrifice.

"Thank you," she whispered to the empty air. "I shall not let your work be wasted."

Outside, Kito was still standing guard at the mouth of the alley, his amber eyes scanning the fog-shrouded street for any sign of danger. When he saw Ada emerge from the house, his ears pricked forward, and his tail gave a single wag of greeting.

"I found it," Ada told him quietly. "I found my second forefather's research. He left me a map to the other things I'll need."

Kito's rumble of approval was almost like words, and Ada could see intelligence shining in his eyes. Now that she knew the truth about his nature, his expressions seemed far more human than they ever had before.

"The Gray family vault," she continued, pulling out her grandfather's journal to consult his notes. "It is hidden beneath the old cemetery, and it contains artifacts that could protect me when I face Malrik. But the journal warns that it shall not be easy to find or easy to enter."

As if in response to her words, the fog around them began to thicken, swirling in patterns that seemed almost purposeful. Ada felt the mark upon her arm begin to tingle with warmth, and she realized that her activities had not gone unnoticed.

Malrik knew she was gathering the tools she would need to challenge him. And he was starting to respond.

"We must move swiftly," Ada said, quickening her pace as they headed toward the old cemetery upon the hill above town. "Before he decides to stop us more directly."

Behind them, the abandoned Thorne house settled back into its watchful silence, its secrets at last passed on to the one they had been meant for. The fog swirled around its walls like protecting arms, as if the spirits of Ada's ancestors were standing guard over the place that had sheltered their knowledge for so many years.

But ahead, in the ancient cemetery where Lowmere's dead had rested for centuries, new dangers waited. The Gray family vault would not give up its secrets easily, and Ada suspected that finding it would require more than merely her grandfather's research.

It would require magic, and courage, and perhaps most importantly, the trust she had built with the spirits who had gone before her.

The fog thickened around them as they climbed the hill toward the cemetery, and Ada could swear she heard whispers carried upon the wind. But whether they were warnings or encouragement, she could not tell.

Either way, she was committed now. The knowledge she carried in her coat, the artifacts she had gathered, the trust of the dead, and the loyalty of the guardian who walked beside her—all of it was leading toward a confrontation that had been building for generations.

Ada pulled her coat tighter around herself and pressed on through the fog, following the path that her ancestors had prepared for her. Behind her, the lights of Lowmere flickered weakly in the mist, as if the town itself was holding its breath.

The final pieces of the puzzle were waiting for her in the cemetery, and once she found them, there would be no turning back.

The curse had shaped her entire life, but now she was at last in a position to shape it in return.

And she would not waste the opportunity her family had died to give her.

Chapter 7:

The Mark of Destiny

The old cemetery sat upon the hill above Lowmere, its crumbling stones circling the town like a crown. Ada had been there only once before when her parents died, and she had hoped never to return. But her grandfather's journal had been clear. Something awaited her there, hidden beneath the Gray family vault, in chambers older than Lowmere itself.

The fog was heavier here than anywhere else, sliding between the headstones as if it possessed a mind of its own. The ancient oaks stretched above her, their branches twisting into strange shapes. The rustle of their leaves sounded too much like whispers. Ada pulled her coat close, trying not to think about how many of the town's lost souls were buried here, or how many had never been found at all.

Kito walked quietly at her side, his amber eyes sharp and alert. He was not merely watching for people. The tension in his body told Ada he sensed something else. Something unseen moving through the fog and the graves.

"The Gray family vault," Ada whispered, checking her grandfather's journal beneath the weak light filtering through the fog. "It should be in the oldest part of the cemetery, marked with their family crest."

But finding it was not easy. The cemetery was much larger up close. Paths twisted and turned in strange ways, and what appeared to be straight trails suddenly curved away when she tried to follow them. Some headstones seemed clear from a distance, but turned worn and unreadable when she drew closer.

After nearly an hour of wandering, Ada seated herself upon a damp, mossy bench to catch her breath. The fog moved around her in slow, swirling patterns, almost as if it possessed a mind of its own. Faint sounds drifted through the air. They were perhaps voices, but they did not sound like the familiar spirits from The Channel. These were older, distant, speaking in languages she did not know.

"We are not going to find it merely by walking about," she said to Kito, who paced beside her, ears twitching. "The journal said the vault was protected by magic. Perhaps I need to use magic to find it."

She took The Channel from her coat and placed it carefully on the bench. Its dark wood gleamed softly in the foggy light, the carved symbols glowing faintly as her fingers touched the wooden plank.

"I'm in need of help," she said quietly. "I seek the Gray family vault, and I cannot find it."

The answer came straightaway, strong and clear, as if someone had been waiting for her to ask.

"Ada," came Elara's familiar voice, warm and steady. "You have done well to come this far. The knowledge you hold now is more than anyone in our family has possessed in generations."

"But I still need the Gray family artifacts," Ada said swiftly. "My second forefather's journal says they are the only things that can protect me when I face Malrik."

"They are," said another voice, a man's this time. His tone was calm but carried a weight of age and sorrow. "I am Marcus Gray, the last of my line. I have waited many years to pass on what we prepared for you."

Ada's pulse quickened. Another ancestor. Another piece of the story falling into place. "You were one of the founders," she said softly. "Your family helped forge the original bargain."

"Aye," Marcus replied, and there was regret in every word. "And every generation since has tried to prepare for the day it could at last be undone. The vault you seek is close by, but it is hidden from normal sight. You shall need to use the mark upon your arm to see it."

Ada glanced down at her forearm, where the faint bell-shaped mark pulsed gently beneath her sleeve. "How do I accomplish this?"

"The mark is more than a symbol," Elara explained. "It is a key created from the magic of all four founding families. When you survived the thirteenth bell as a child, it awakened that power within you. The power our family has carried in silence for generations."

Ada rolled up her sleeve and gazed at the mark upon her arm. In the dim light of the cemetery, it seemed to glow of its own accord, its edges sharper and brighter than she had ever seen before.

"I do not understand," she said quietly. "Why me? Why was I chosen when so many others came before me?"

The silence that followed felt deep and heavy. When the spirits at last spoke again, their voices carried a weight that made Ada's chest tighten.

"Because you are the last," Marcus said softly. "The final descendant of the direct bloodlines. After you, there shall be no one else with the power to stand against the curse."

"But there is more to it than that," Elara added. "You were prepared for this before you were even born. While you grew in your mother's womb, the surviving members of our families joined together and placed a blessing on you. It was meant to protect you from the full strength of the curse and give you abilities that none of us ever possessed."

Ada pressed her hand against the mark and felt its warmth spread up her arm and into her chest. "What kind of abilities?" she asked.

"The power to walk between worlds," said a new voice. Kito's ears twitched as if he recognized it. "The power to command the spirits as well as speak with them. The power to face Malrik as his equal in his own realm."

This voice sounded different from the others. It was younger, stronger, and seemed to stand closer to the living world than the rest.

"Who are you?" Ada asked, her voice trembling.

"I am Jonathan Thorne," the voice answered, and Ada's breath caught. "I have been watching over you since the day you were born, waiting for the moment when you would be ready to accept your destiny."

Tears filled Ada's eyes. Hearing her grandfather's voice, knowing that he had been there all along, brought a warmth she had not felt since her parents died.

"I found your journal. Your research. It led me here," she whispered.

"As it was meant to," Jonathan said with quiet pride. "You have done well, Ada. Better than I hoped when I realized my time was running short. The knowledge you have gathered, the artifacts you carry, the trust you have built with the spirits—all of it has prepared you for what comes next."

"But I am afraid," Ada admitted. "Three others tried before me and failed. How can I succeed where they could not?"

"Because they lacked what you possess," Marcus said firmly. "They had pieces of the puzzle, small fragments of knowledge and power. You have the complete picture. The Channel is fully restored, the blessing in your blood is fully awakened, and you have the support of all the founding families together."

"And there is something else you understand that they did not," Elara added. "The mark upon your arm is not a burden or a curse. It is a gift, earned through generations of sacrifice. When you cease fighting it and accept what you truly are, your power shall become whole."

Ada gazed down at the mark again, and for the first time in seven years, she felt something other than shame when she saw it. The bell-shaped outline appeared beautiful now, not strange or frightening but full of purpose. Its lines seemed to glow softly, alive with meaning. A gentle warmth spread from her arm through her whole body, filling her with strength and calm she had never known before. It was as if the mark itself had been waiting for this moment.

"How do I use it to find the vault?" she asked quietly, her voice steady despite the rush of energy within her.

"Place your marked hand upon the stone beneath you," Jonathan said. "The bench upon which you sit was carved from the same rock as the vault's foundation. Let your power move through it, and it shall show you where to go."

Ada pressed her palm flat against the moss-covered bench, and the world around her changed at once. The fog seemed to draw back, swept away by an unseen wind, and the cemetery came into focus like a painting sharpening before her eyes. Every headstone and tree stood out with crystal clarity.

But what truly caught her breath were the glowing lines that appeared in the ground, faint but alive, running between the graves. They shimmered like threads of light, weaving through the cemetery in patterns that joined to form a vast, magical design.

At the center of that design, directly ahead of her, stood a headstone that had not been there a moment earlier. It was larger than all the others, made of black granite that seemed to drink in the light rather than reflect it. At its crown was a carved crest exactly like the one she had seen in her grandfather's journal. It was a great tree whose roots sank deep into the earth and whose branches reached toward the stars. The sight made Ada's chest tighten with awe.

"I can see it," she whispered, rising slowly from the bench. "I can see the Gray family marker."

"Touch the crest," Marcus said gently. "Let your mark meet the stone, and the way shall open for you."

Ada picked up The Channel and tucked it safely inside her coat before moving toward the headstone, her steps careful and reverent. Kito walked beside her, his head low, his muscles tense but calm. His golden eyes glowed faintly in the strange light. He was not growling this time. He seemed to understand that what waited ahead was not danger but destiny.

Ada placed her hand upon the crest. The instant her marked skin met the cool granite, the stone came alive beneath her fingers. Warmth spread through it, and she heard a deep, rumbling sound far below, like ancient gears turning after centuries of silence.

The ground before the headstone began to tremble. Cracks spread outward, widening slowly until the soil split apart. Dust and roots fell away, and from the darkness below rose a staircase carved from the same black granite as the marker. The steps spiraled downward into shadow, but Ada saw a faint golden glow at the bottom, as if lanterns waited to guide her path.

"The vault is protected by more than the magic that hides it," Elara warned gently. "Guardians rest below, spirits bound to defend what is kept there. But they shall know you by your mark and allow you to pass."

Ada nodded, feeling the weight of the moment settle upon her shoulders like a cloak. She took a deep breath and stepped forward. Her fingers brushed the smooth stone wall as she began to descend, the cold surface steady beneath her touch.

Kito followed close behind, silent but alert, his claws clicking softly against the granite steps. The deeper they went, the colder the air became, though it was not the cold of fear. It felt different—peaceful, ancient, like a long-forgotten welcome. The chill wrapped around her like a familiar hand guiding her home.

At length, the stairs ended in a wide circular chamber lit by torches that burned with steady, pale flames. They cast light but no shadows, filling the room with an even glow that made every detail clear. The walls were carved with images that told stories in stone. Scenes of the Gray family, their rise, their sorrow, and their part in founding Lowmere. Each carving seemed to move slightly in the torchlight, as if alive with memory.

But what drew Ada's eyes most was at the center of the room.

A white marble pedestal stood there, shining softly, and upon it rested three objects that made the mark upon her arm tingle with recognition. The first was a cloak that shimmered like liquid silver, its color shifting to black whenever she blinked. Beside it lay a sword whose blade gleamed as if lit from within, its edge sharp and bright with power. And resting above both was a crown made from threads of light, as though moonbeams themselves had been woven together.

Ada's breath caught. She knew deep in her heart that these were the artifacts her grandfather had written about. The treasures of the Gray family, meant for her, meant for this moment.

It was not the sword or the crown that drew Ada forward, but the fourth object resting at the edge of the pedestal. It was a small wooden box, plain and smooth, no larger than her hand. Strange symbols were carved across its surface, the same ones that glowed faintly upon The Channel. Despite its simple appearance, Ada could feel the power emanating from it, quiet but strong, like a heartbeat hidden beneath the surface.

"The Gray family's greatest creation," Marcus said, his voice resounding directly within her mind. "This box holds the essence of protection itself. When you open it in the realm of Moorlow, it shall guard you against Malrik's strongest attacks."

Ada picked it up carefully. The wood was warm beneath her fingertips, lighter than she expected, almost weightless. The moment her skin touched it, a wave of energy spread through her body, connecting her mark to the magic surrounding her. The feeling was not painful, but rather it was alive, pulsing through her like sunlight beneath her skin.

"Take the cloak as well," Marcus continued. "It shall hide you from those who wish you harm and turn away attacks meant to wound you. The sword and crown must remain here for another time, another descendant. But these two shall serve you well in the battle ahead."

Ada nodded, her heart steady now. She lifted the shimmering cloak and wrapped it around her shoulders. The fabric was softer than silk and seemed to hum with quiet power. The moment it touched her, her vision sharpened. The shadows in the chamber grew clearer, edges brighter, every flicker of light suddenly more alive. When she gazed down, she could scarcely see herself at all. Her hands and arms were faint outlines, fading into the air.

"It's like the fog," she whispered. "I am part of it."

"Now go," came Jonathan's gentle voice. "Return to the surface and prepare for what is coming. These artifacts are tools, Ada. They shall protect you, but your true strength lies in what you are, in the blessing that sets you apart."

With a final glance at the pedestal and the treasures left behind, Ada turned toward the staircase. Kito remained close at her side as they began the long climb upward. The stone walls glowed faintly with the same lines of energy she had seen before, guiding her like soft light through the darkness.

When they reached the surface, the last step sealed itself behind them with a sound like a sigh. The cracks in the ground closed, and the Gray family headstone appeared ordinary once more. Only Ada's racing heart knew what lay beneath.

She stood there for a moment, breathing in the heavy night air. The cemetery was silent save for the wind whispering through the trees. She was about to step away when something shifted in the fog.

Footsteps. Slow, steady, deliberate.

Then came voices, low and cold, their words cutting through the mist like knives.

"She was here," said one, the sound seeming to come from everywhere at once. "The marked one. Her power yet lingers."

Ada froze. The warmth from her mark faded, replaced by a chill that sank deep into her bones. She pulled the cloak tight around herself and crouched low behind a tall headstone. Kito pressed close beside her, silent but tense, his fur bristling.

Through the fog, shapes began to appear. Tall, thin figures moved between the graves, their pale skin almost glowing in the moonlight. Their eyes shimmered with an icy blue light that made Ada's heart pound. They moved too smoothly, too quietly, as if gliding rather than walking.

"Malrik's servants," Ada whispered to herself, her voice barely audible. "He has sent them to find me."

The figures spread out across the cemetery, their movements precise and eerie. Ada could hear them speaking in low voices that carried through the fog like distant echoes.

"The barriers grow thin," one said, its tone like metal scraping stone. "Soon the master shall send more of us through."

"Find the girl," another ordered. "The one with the mark. Bring her back alive. The master has plans for her."

Ada's pulse quickened. If she had reached the vault even a few minutes later, she would have walked straight into their hands. She swallowed hard, forcing her breath to remain quiet.

She began to move. Step by step, she slipped through the cemetery, keeping low, her cloak blending her into the mist. Every sound seemed deafening to her ears, the crunch of pebbles, the soft rustle of grass, even the faint swish of her cloak as it brushed the ground.

Kito moved beside her, every muscle in his body taut. His ears twitched at sounds Ada could not hear, and more than once, he nudged her away from a path that appeared safe but was not. His instincts were sharper than her eyes; he seemed to sense the presence of the pale figures even when they were hidden.

It felt like hours before the iron gates came into view through the thick fog. They were old and rusted, their hinges moaning softly as the wind passed through. Ada paused, waiting as one of the figures turned its head sharply in her direction. She held her breath, willing herself to be invisible. The figure's glowing eyes swept across the space where she hid, lingered for a heartbeat, and then moved on.

Only when it turned away did Ada take another step.

Slowly, painstakingly, she reached the gates and slipped through, her cloak brushing against the cold metal. The moment she and Kito crossed into the street beyond, a strange calm fell over her. The fog of the cemetery remained behind them, heavy and watchful, as if unwilling to let them go.

By the time they reached the cliffs, Ada was trembling with exhaustion. Her legs ached, her hands were cold, but her heart burned with determination. She had what she came for. The Gray family artifacts, her grandfather's research, and The Channel together gave her everything she needed to face Malrik in his realm.

Almost everything.

One last truth remained for her to accept. The spirits had tried to tell her again and again, but only now did she begin to understand. The mark upon her arm was not a curse or a punishment. It was a gift, a blessing left behind by generations who had sacrificed everything for this moment.

As Ada walked through the fog-covered streets of Lowmere, the box held safely beneath her cloak, she felt the mark pulse warmly against her skin. For the first time in seven years, the feeling did not fill her with guilt or fear.

It felt like hope.

Behind her, the pale figures searched through the graves, unaware that their prey had already escaped with treasures their master could never replace. Ahead of her, upon the cliffs where her journey had begun, the faint light of her cottage waited in the mist.

The blessing was complete. The tools were gathered.

And Ada Thorne, marked by the past, chosen by the spirits, and armed by her ancestors, was at last ready to face the Bellringer and end the curse that had haunted Lowmere for centuries. She was the last hope of the founding families. The one meant to break the chain. The girl who would save her town, or die in the attempt.

Chapter 8:

On the Edge of Darkness

Ada sat upon the same stretch of rocky beach where everything had changed. The sea stretched endlessly before her, its surface restless beneath a sky that could never quite decide whether it was dusk or dawn. The fog rolled in thick waves, swallowing the horizon, while the setting sun struggled to paint faint streaks of silver and gray across the mist. The air smelled of salt, old stone, and rain that had not yet fallen.

She drew her knees to her chest, the rough pebbles pressing into her legs through her worn garments. Each sound around her—the relentless crash of waves, the hollow cry of distant gulls, the faint clatter of pebbles shifting beneath the tide—seemed sharper tonight, as if the world were listening to her breathe.

Kito lay close beside her, his thick fur brushing against her arm. His amber eyes glowed faintly in the dim light, catching the reflection of the sea like two small lanterns. Every now and then, he let out a low rumble, not in warning but in something that felt almost like thought. He was her only companion, her constant shadow through nights that had been colder and darker than this one.

The same beach had held her when she had fled from the townsfolk's stares and whispers, when her heart had broken beneath the weight of blame she did not deserve. That night yet lived within her, the way she had stumbled barefoot over the rocks, the fog curling around her like a living thing, and the sound of the thirteenth bell ringing through the dark. That was when she had first heard the voices in the mist calling her name. Back then, she had thought she was losing her mind. Now she knew better.

Only a few nights had passed since then, but it felt like years. Every moment since the bell had tolled had reshaped her understanding of who she was. The voices, the mark, the curse—they were threads in a story she had inherited long before she was born. And now that story had chosen her to finish it.

The waves rolled in closer, licking at the stones near her feet. Ada rested her chin upon her knees and stared out at the sea. It no longer appeared ordinary to her eyes. Every crest that rose and broke carried a whisper of something ancient beneath it. Every dip between waves shimmered faintly with a light only she could see, like the hidden heartbeat of the ocean itself.

She thought of the drawings in her grandfather's journal, the ships dashed against invisible rocks, the fishermen who never returned. "It used to be so much worse," she murmured, almost to herself. "Before the bargain. Before Malrik."

The words were carried away on the wind, but Kito's ears flicked toward her. He shifted, stretching out beside her, his massive head resting against her leg. Ada smiled faintly and ran her fingers through the coarse fur behind his ears.

"They thought they were saving everyone," she said quietly. "The founding families. They were terrified, watching people vanish into the sea every week, begging the waves for mercy. When Malrik came, they saw a savior, not a monster. One life each New Moon seemed like a mercy compared to losing dozens. But they did not think about what they were truly inviting in."

She could almost see it as she spoke: The night of the bargain, the villagers gathered upon the cliffs with lanterns flickering in the wind, their faces pale with desperation. Malrik rising from the mist, half-man, half-shadow, his voice like the low hum of a bell rolling across the sea. She imagined her ancestors' fear, their hands shaking as they signed away generations of peace for one fleeting promise of safety.

Ada picked up a smooth, flat stone from the beach and turned it over in her hands. The surface was cool, slick with moisture, its shape worn down by countless tides. "They did not mean to curse us," she said softly. "They were only trying to survive."

She threw the stone out over the water and watched it disappear with a small splash. Ripples spread outward, then vanished into the restless surface. The sea did not even seem to notice.

Her mark tingled beneath her sleeve, a soft pulse that matched the rhythm of her heartbeat. She rolled up her arm to gaze at it. In the fading light, the bell-shaped outline glowed faintly, as if it were alive beneath her skin. The sight did not fill her with dread anymore; it made her chest ache with something like pride.

"I used to hate this," she whispered. "I thought it made me cursed. But perhaps it means I am still here because I was meant to be."

Kito lifted his head and made a sound deep in his throat, half-growl, half-hum. His eyes met hers, steady and knowing. In them, Ada saw not merely an animal but a guardian, one who had watched generations live and die waiting for her moment to come.

"You have been waiting for this, haven't you?" she asked softly. "For someone who could end it at last."

Kito blinked slowly, then rested his head back upon her leg, as if in quiet agreement.

The tide crept higher, the waves brushing her boots with cold foam that glowed faintly beneath the twilight. Ada stood and walked closer to the water's edge, her breath clouding in the chill air. The horizon was hidden now, swallowed by fog. Yet her vision, sharpened by the blessing in her blood, could see what lay beyond—the shimmer of another world layered over this one. Shadows moved beneath the surface of the waves, slow and sinuous, and lights flickered deep below, forming patterns that felt almost intelligent.

And in that unseen world beyond, she felt Malrik's presence.

It was not sight or sound but a pull, like gravity itself bending toward her. He was there, just beyond reach, watching her.

"I can feel him," she said beneath her breath, her voice trembling but resolute. "He knows I am coming."

The wind rose sharply, carrying the faint scent of salt and something older, something that reminded her of crypts and forgotten prayers. Ada wrapped the Gray cloak tighter around herself, its magic humming faintly in response.

Kito stood beside her now, the fur along his spine bristling, his ears pricked forward toward the sea. Together, they faced the darkness gathering upon the horizon.

This time, Ada did not flinch.

"Even from here, I can feel him watching. He knows I possess The Channel now. He knows I have gathered the artifacts and learned the truth about my heritage. He is waiting for me to make my move."

A cold wind moved through the air, laced with salt and the faint scent of damp earth. It carried a whisper of decay, the kind that lingered in old graves and long-lost memories. Ada drew the Gray cloak tighter still, its fabric shielding her from both the night's chill and the unseen eyes that watched her.

"The spirits said I am the last chance," she continued, speaking as much to herself as to Kito. "The final descendant of the founding families with the power to break the curse. If I fail, there will not be anyone else to try. Lowmere will perish, and Malrik's hunger shall spread to other towns, other coasts, until there is nothing left but empty shells and blowing sand."

The thought should have terrified her, and part of it did. But underneath the fear was something stronger, something that had been growing within her ever since she first spoke to the spirits through The Channel. Purpose. For the first time in her life, she knew exactly why she existed, exactly what she was meant to do.

"I am no longer Ada the outcast," she said, her voice growing stronger. "I am not merely the girl who survived when she should not have. I am Ada Thorne, daughter of the founding families, chosen by blood and blessing to face the darkness. And I am going to end this."

Ada turned away from the sea and gazed back toward Lowmere, its lights flickering weakly through the fog like dying stars. The town appeared so small from here, so fragile. It was hard to believe that such a humble place could be the center of a conflict that had been building for generations.

But she could see the truth now, could understand how the curse had shaped every aspect of life in Lowmere. The fear that kept people indoors upon New Moon nights. The superstitions that governed their daily routines. The way they gazed at her with a mixture of dread and blame, as if her very existence was a reminder of their helplessness against forces beyond their control.

"They have been living in the shadow of the curse for so long that they have forgotten what it means to hope," she said. "They accept the disappearances as inevitable, part of the natural order. But it does not have to be that way. The bargain can be broken. The curse can be ended."

Ada began walking back toward her cottage, Kito padding silently beside her. The artifacts she had gathered over the past week were safely hidden in her home, waiting for the moment when she would need them: The Channel, her grandfather's journal, the Gray family's protective items, and most importantly, the knowledge she had gained from speaking with the spirits of her ancestors.

Everything she needed to challenge Malrik in his own realm was at last within her grasp. But as she climbed the narrow path that led up from the beach, Ada felt the weight of what lay ahead settling upon her shoulders like a physical burden.

She would have to enter Moorlow, the shadow realm where the Bellringer held court over the souls of the missing. She would have to face a creature that had been growing stronger for generations, feeding upon the fear and despair of her people. And she would have to do it knowing that three others had tried before her and failed, each attempt making the curse more dangerous and unpredictable.

"But I have advantages they did not," she reminded herself, echoing what the spirits had told her. "The complete Channel, the full blessing, the support of all the founding families. And most importantly, I understand what they did not. This is not merely about breaking a bargain or destroying a monster. It is about healing a wound that has been festering for generations."

Ada paused at her garden gate and gazed back once more at the sea. The last traces of sunlight had faded from the sky, and the water stretched away into darkness that seemed to go on forever. But she was no longer afraid of that darkness. She understood it now, knew it for what it truly was.

Not an enemy to be fought, but a problem to be solved.

"Tomorrow night," she said quietly, "the New Moon rises, and Malrik shall toll his bell again. But this time, instead of taking someone from Lowmere, he shall have to face someone who is ready to fight back."

Ada opened her garden gate and walked up the path to her cottage, where warm lamplight glowed in the windows and The Channel waited upon her kitchen table. She had spent years fleeing from her destiny, years trying to be something other than what she was born to be.

But those days were over.

Within her cottage, Ada lit the candles that surrounded The Channel and placed her hands on the familiar surface of the heart-shaped plank. The connection came instantly, stronger than it had ever been before, as if the spirits were waiting eagerly for her call.

"I am ready," she said simply.

The response was immediate, a chorus of voices that filled her small cottage with warmth and light.

"We know," said Elara's voice, filled with pride and affection. "We have felt your acceptance, your understanding of what you truly are. The blessing in your blood sings with power now, and the mark upon your arm blazes like a star."

"Tomorrow night," added Jonathan's voice, "when the thirteenth bell tolls, you shall answer its call. But instead of fleeing or hiding, you shall step forward and claim your birthright as the last hope of the founding families."

"The tools you carry shall protect you," said Marcus Gray. "The knowledge you have gained shall guide you. But your greatest strength shall come from within, from at last embracing the truth that you are not cursed but chosen."

Ada felt tears running down her cheeks, but they were tears of joy rather than sorrow. For the first time in seven years, she felt truly connected to something larger than herself. Not merely the spirits who spoke to her through The Channel, but the entire history of her people, stretching back to the desperate founders who had made their terrible bargain with the sea.

"I will not let you down," she promised. "I will not let any of you down."

"We know," said Tam Fletcher's gentle voice, "because you are stronger than fear, braver than despair, and more powerful than the darkness that threatens to consume us all."

The voices faded gradually, leaving Ada alone in her cottage with only the sound of the wind outside her windows and the steady breathing of Kito by her feet. But the silence did not feel empty anymore. It felt expectant, full of possibility and potential.

Ada gazed around her cottage one more time, taking in the simple furnishings and familiar objects that had been her whole world for so long. Tomorrow, she would leave this place and enter a realm beyond imagination, where the laws of physics bent to the will of supernatural forces and the very air was thick with magic and danger.

She might not return. The three who had tried before her had all died in the attempt, their souls claimed by the very creature they had sought to defeat. But even if she failed, even if she joined their ranks in Malrik's prison, she would face her fate with courage and dignity.

Because she at last understood what she was.

Not a victim of the curse, but its destined destroyer.

Not an outcast marked by tragedy, but a chosen one blessed by love.

Not the last of a dying bloodline, but the first of something new.

Ada Thorne, daughter of the founding families, guardian of Lowmere's future, and the only hope her people had left.

She blew out the candles surrounding The Channel and carefully wrapped the board in its protective cloth. Tomorrow night, she would use it one final time to open the way into Moorlow and begin the confrontation that would determine the fate of her town.

But tonight, she would rest and gather her strength for the battle ahead.

Outside, the fog rolled in from the sea as it had every night for generations, carrying with it the whispers of the dead and the promises of the damned. But Ada no longer feared those whispers.

She was ready to add her own voice to the chorus.

And when she did, the very foundations of Malrik's power would tremble.

The curse that had plagued Lowmere for generations was about to meet its match in a girl who had at last learned to embrace her destiny.

The darkness had ruled long enough.

It was time for the light to fight back.

Chapter 9:

The Confrontation

The clock upon the mantel struck midnight, each chime slow and heavy, echoing through the fog that pressed against the cottage walls. Ada sat cross-legged upon the floor, directly beneath the window, The Channel spread out on a worn blanket that had once belonged to her grandmother. The fabric smelled faintly of smoke and lavender, and for some reason, that made her chest tighten.

Kito lay close beside her, head resting on his paws but eyes wide open, their amber glow catching the candlelight. His ears twitched at sounds Ada could not hear. Outside, the fog swallowed everything. It was the kind of night that made even familiar places feel wrong, still and cold in a way that crept beneath one's skin.

It was not merely the weather. Ada could feel something else in the air tonight, something that did not belong. The silence was too perfect, too complete. No wind. No insects. Not even the faint crash of waves upon the rocks below. It was as if the whole world was holding its breath.

From her window, she could see nothing but a wall of gray mist. Every now and then, a flicker of light broke through the fog, lightning that flashed without sound. And in that light, shadows moved. Not people—at least, not anymore. Their shapes were wrong. They drifted instead of walking, bending at unnatural angles.

Ada tried not to gaze at them. She had been sitting there for nearly an hour, gathering her courage for what she knew would be her last attempt to reach the other side before everything began. Her hands rested upon her knees, trembling no matter how tightly she clenched them. Tomorrow night, when the New Moon rose, she would cross into Moorlow itself. Tonight, she would speak to the one who ruled it.

She reached out and brushed her fingers across The Channel's surface. The dark wood gleamed in the candlelight, and the faint symbols carved into it seemed to shimmer as if alive. The plank sat waiting, its smooth surface reflecting her pale face.

Kito gave a low sound deep in his throat—a warning perhaps, or merely fear.

Ada swallowed hard. "You feel it as well, don't you?" she whispered. "He draws near."

The hyena did not move, but his muscles tensed beneath his coat, ready to spring. Ada wished she could take comfort in his presence, but the air around them felt thick, charged, alive in the worst manner.

She placed her hands on the heart-shaped plank. The wood was icy, colder than it should have been, and the cold crawled up her arms instantly. Her breath hitched. It felt like holding something alive, something that did not wish to be touched.

But she did not pull away.

Her voice shook at first, but she forced the words out nonetheless.

"Malrik. I know you can hear me. You have been watching me, have you not? Watching while I gather everything your servants tried to destroy. I am no longer hiding."

For a moment, nothing happened. Then, one by one, the candles went out.

The darkness that followed was thick, swallowing everything. The temperature dropped so abruptly that her lungs burned when she breathed. Frost spread across the inside of the window, crackling softly as it formed, and Ada's breath came out in pale clouds that hung in the air like ghosts.

The plank jerked to life with violent force, nearly pulling Ada's hands from the board entirely. When it began to move, it spelled out words in letters so sharp and angular they seemed to cut through the air itself.

"S-O Y-O-U H-A-V-E F-O-U-N-D Y-O-U-R V-O-I-C-E A-T L-A-S-T"

Then came the sound.

At first, she thought it was the wind. A faint whisper, distant and low. But it grew, rising from the corners of the room, from beneath the floorboards, from within the walls themselves. Laughter. Cold, sharp laughter that did not belong to anything human.

The plank twitched beneath her fingers. Once. Twice. Then it started to move of its own accord, swift enough to burn her palms. She smelled something acrid and realized it was her own skin scorching against the frozen wood. Yet she did not let go.

The laughter stopped as suddenly as it had begun. The silence that followed was worse. And then a voice filled it.

"Little marked child," it hissed. The words seemed to slide through the dark like oil, slipping into her ears, her head, her thoughts. "Little broken thing pretending to be brave. You dare summon me as though I were one of your whispering ancestors? You dare speak my name as though it belongs in your mouth?"

Ada's breath caught. Her heart was pounding so hard she could feel it in her fingertips. The plank jerked violently, racing across the board faster than she could follow, leaving faint streaks of light behind it. But the voice was not coming from the board anymore. It was within her, within her mind, every word pounding through her skull like hammer blows.

Ada opened her mouth to scream, but her voice would not come. The sound of him, the way his words crawled through her mind, was worse than anything she had imagined. It was not merely a voice; it was a presence, a cold weight pressing down upon every inch of her being.

"You have been busy, have you not?" Malrik said, his tone almost playful. "Running through graveyards, whispering to ghosts, collecting trinkets from dead families. All that work, and yet you tremble like a frightened child."

The plank spun wildly beneath her palms, circling faster and faster until it slammed against the edge of the board. Ada flinched, her breath ragged.

"Why are you afraid, little one?" the voice purred. "You have touched power, have you not? You have tasted it. But you do not yet understand it. Power is not meant for you. It is meant for those strong enough to take it, not for small, trembling things that pretend to be heroes."

Ada clenched her teeth, fighting through the ice crawling up her arms. Her mark burned hot beneath her sleeve, a faint light pulsing through the fabric.

"I am not pretending," she said, forcing the words through the pain. "I know what I am now. And I know what you have done."

Malrik laughed again, soft and low this time, like the sea on a calm night. "What *I* have done? I kept your town alive. I gave your people peace when the ocean would have swallowed them whole. They begged for my aid. I gave it freely. It is not my fault they paid a price they could not bear."

"You preyed upon them," Ada said. Her voice shook, but it held strong. "You took their lives, their fear. You built a prison of souls beneath the sea and called it salvation."

The shadows in the room thickened, gathering near the corners until they appeared almost solid. The window glass rattled. Kito growled low, every hair upon his body raised.

"Brave words," Malrik said. "You sound just like the ones who came before you. They all said the same thing—at first. Then they begged."

Ada's throat tightened. She thought of the three who had tried before her, their names etched in her grandfather's journal. Each had gone into Moorlow. None had returned.

"What did you do to them?" she whispered.

Malrik chuckled. "They are here with me. Would you like to hear them?"

Before Ada could answer, the air filled with voices. They rose all at once, overlapping, pleading, sobbing, calling her name. She recognized one. Tam Fletcher. His voice came through clearer than the rest, desperate and broken.

"Ada," it said, "do not come here. Do not—"

His voice cut off.

Her eyes filled with tears she did not notice until they froze upon her lashes. She gritted her teeth, pressing her hands harder upon the plank. "You cannot frighten me."

"Oh, but I can," Malrik hissed. "You simply do not know how deep fear runs yet. You think you carry courage because of that mark upon your arm. But the mark does not make you chosen. It makes you mine."

Something within Ada snapped. The fear did not vanish, but it twisted into something else, something fierce.

"No," she said. "It does not belong to you."

The mark upon her arm flared with light, bright enough to cut through the darkness. The glow spread down her wrist and into her fingertips, flooding the board with a soft gold hue. The plank stopped moving.

Malrik hissed, a sound like the ocean striking stone. "Foolish girl."

"You have held your dominion over this place long enough," Ada said, her voice shaking but strong. "You have hidden behind bargains and fear, but it ends now. Tomorrow night, I come to you."

The laughter that followed was sharp and ugly. "You? Come to me?"

The shadows near the window began to twist and rise, shaping into the faint outline of a figure. The fog outside thickened until it pressed against the glass like a living thing. "You shall drown before you take a single step into my realm. Do you think your little spirits can save you? They cannot even save themselves."

The candles flickered back to life, one by one, though Ada had not moved. Their flames burned blue instead of gold, casting a ghostly light across the room.

"I will find you," she said quietly. "And I will end this."

The voice laughed once more, but this time it sounded strained, almost uncertain. "You are too small to understand what you threaten. Break the bell, and the sea shall rise again. The world you cling to shall drown, child. There is no victory for you, only different kinds of ruin."

Ada's heart hammered, but she met the darkness head-on. "Then I shall choose ruin," she said.

The plank jerked hard enough to break from her grip. It clattered to the floor, the sound sharp in the heavy silence that followed.

Then, nothing. The shadows retreated. The frost upon the window began to melt. The candles steadied, their flames turning warm again.

Kito whined softly and pressed his head against Ada's shoulder. She was shaking, her palms raw and red where the cold had bitten into her skin. For a long time, she could not move. She merely sat there in the candlelight, staring at the motionless board.

Her whole body ached, but her mind was clear. She had spoken to Malrik and survived. Barely, but she had.

When she stood at last, her legs felt unsteady. She reached down, picked up the fallen plank, and set it carefully on the board. The Channel's surface glimmered faintly, as if the encounter had left a mark upon it as well.

Kito watched her as she wrapped the board in its cloth again. His gaze was steady, loyal. He had no need for words. They both knew what came next. Tomorrow night, she would go into the dark. This time, she was not going to flee from it.

Ada tied the cloth around The Channel with deliberate care, the fabric trembling slightly in her hands. She could still feel Malrik's presence, like a shadow that had not quite left the room, but the weight of it was thinner now, less certain. The mark upon her arm glowed faintly through her sleeve, warm rather than burning.

Kito moved closer, his claws clicking softly on the floorboards. He nosed at her arm as if to test that she was still whole. Ada let out a shaky laugh and scratched behind his ears, the simple motion grounding her. "I am well," she whispered. Her voice was rough, but it did not waver. "I am well."

She stood and crossed to the window. The fog pressed close to the glass, but now it felt different. Not empty, not waiting. More like something had shifted on the other side, a door opened, or a line crossed. Ada laid her palm flat against the cold pane and closed her eyes. She could feel Moorlow out there, just beyond the veil. It was like gazing at the ocean and realizing you were looking at an entire world beneath the waves.

The spirits stirred. She did not hear their voices at first, merely a low hum that vibrated through the wood of the window frame and the floor beneath her feet. Then, softly, they began to speak. Familiar voices. Elara's, warm and steady. Marcus Gray's, clipped but proud. And behind them, Jonathan Thorne, her grandfather, quiet but present, like a hand resting upon her shoulder.

"You have done what no one else could," Elara said, her tone threaded with approval. "You have gazed into the heart of Moorlow and survived."

"He is not as strong as he thinks," Marcus added. "He has been feeding upon fear for so long that he has forgotten what defiance feels like."

Jonathan's voice followed, low and certain. "You have forced him to see you, Ada. Not as a frightened child, but as what you are. The last of us. The one we built this for."

Ada pressed her forehead to the cold glass. Tears pricked at her eyes, but she did not let them fall. "I felt him," she whispered. "He is... vast. Like a storm, like the sea itself. How do I fight something like that?"

"You do not fight him as a mortal," Elara said gently. "You fight him as what you have become."

Ada opened her eyes. The mark upon her arm had begun to pulse again, brighter now, the glow bleeding through the cloth of her sleeve. She could feel it spreading through her, filling the space where fear had dwelt a moment before.

Jonathan spoke again. "Tomorrow, you shall cross the threshold. Moorlow shall try to twist you, break you. But you carry every blessing, every fragment of power that our families poured into your bloodline. You are not walking into the dark alone. We are with you."

Kito made a low, rumbling sound and brushed against her leg. Ada rested her hand upon his back. "And he?" she asked.

"He is more than a guardian," Marcus said. "He is the oldest promise we made. He has watched over every Thorne who bore the mark, waiting for this night."

Ada turned back to the room and slowly knelt beside The Channel again. The wooden plank sat motionless upon the board, but the symbols carved into the wood still glimmered faintly, responding to her touch. She traced them with her fingertips, feeling the hum of power beneath the surface.

"This is it, then," she said softly. "No more fleeing."

"No more fleeing," Jonathan echoed. "You have already begun to break his hold. That is why he sent the voices of the lost to you. He fears you."

Ada let out a breath she had not realized she had been holding. The fear was there, it probably always would be, but something stronger sat beneath it now, a steady pulse like a heartbeat. Purpose.

She reached for the cloak draped over the back of the chair and swung it over her shoulders. Its silver-black folds settled around her like a second skin, cool but comforting. The edges shimmered faintly, almost invisible in the dim candlelight. She could feel its magic working, wrapping her in quiet strength.

Kito rose to his feet, his muscles rippling beneath his coat. Ada stroked his neck once, then stood, pulling the cloak tighter. "Tomorrow night," she murmured, gazing past the window into the rolling fog. "I come to you on my own terms."

Outside, the lightning flickered again, but this time Ada thought she saw the mist recoil slightly from the flash, as if something within it had drawn back. She felt the mark pulse against her skin, not in pain but in power, like a signal sent out into the night.

"We are ready," she whispered.

The spirits did not answer this time. They had no need to. The hum of their presence faded, leaving only the quiet of the cottage and Kito's steady breathing. Ada turned toward her small bed. She would not sleep much, but she would try. Tomorrow, she would leave this room, perhaps forever, and step into the realm of Moorlow to face Malrik where he ruled.

She crossed to her bedside table and blew out the last candle. Darkness swept the room, soft and complete, but for the first time, it did not feel hostile. It felt like a pause. Like a held breath before a final plunge.

Ada lay down, one hand resting on the mark beneath her sleeve. The warmth of it soothed her. Kito curled up upon the rug at her feet, his eyes closing slowly, ears pricked.

Tomorrow night, she thought. *The New Moon rises. The bell tolls again. And this time, someone will answer.*

Ada did not lie down straightaway. She tried, but the stillness pressed too hard against her chest. Every sound, every flicker of wind outside, made her nerves jump. The fog brushed against the windows like restless fingers, and somewhere beyond the cliffs, the faint toll of a bell echoed once. Not the cursed one, not yet, but a true bell, the old chapel's midnight chime carried thinly through the mist. Even so, it made her blood run cold.

Kito's ears pricked at the sound. He lifted his head and gave a soft, uneasy growl, then rested it again, never taking his eyes from the window.

Ada stood, unable to keep still. Her thoughts would not quiet. Every word Malrik had spoken crawled through her mind, the sneer in his tone, the confidence, the way he had claimed her mark as his. He had sounded so sure, so ancient.

Yet beneath that arrogance, she had heard something else. A tremor. The faintest flicker of fear.

"He is afraid," she said aloud, surprising herself. Her voice came out low, steady. "He knows what approaches."

She crossed to her small desk, where her grandfather's journal lay open to the final pages. The ink had faded over time, but she knew every line by heart. Her grandfather's handwriting was looping, deliberate, each word filled with intent. *If the mark awakens fully, the bell shall call to its bearer. Follow it. Fear not the sound. It is not death's call, it is the door.*

Her fingers brushed over the line. "The door," she murmured. "So that is how I find it."

The mark upon her arm pulsed in response, the light spreading outward like ripples in water. She rolled up her sleeve and watched as the faint golden glow danced over her skin. It was beautiful in a strange, almost mournful way, a reminder of everything she had lost and everything she was about to risk.

Kito stirred and rose to his feet. His claws clicked against the floorboards as he came to stand beside her. She gazed down at him and managed a small smile. "It is almost time," she said. "You can feel it as well, can't you?"

He gave a soft rumble, neither confirming nor denying, more like understanding.

Ada reached for The Channel again, unwrapping the cloth one last time. The board gleamed faintly, as if it remembered what had just occurred. She did not touch the plank this time. Instead, she laid her marked hand flat against the surface. The symbols began to glow, faint gold lines tracing outward in a spiral, forming patterns she had never noticed before, runes hidden beneath the runes. The wood vibrated beneath her palm, humming softly, and then, clear and unmistakable, she heard her grandfather's voice.

"Courage, my Ada," Jonathan said, his tone warm and steady. "You have awakened the line. Every name, every soul tied to our blood stands with you now. Do not forget that when you walk into the dark."

More voices joined his—Elara, Marcus, others she did not recognize—all whispering words she could not quite make out, but their presence filled the room like light breaking through fog. The air shimmered faintly, and Ada's hair lifted with the charge that rippled through it.

Tears burned at the corners of her eyes. "I do not know if I can prevail," she whispered.

"You can," Elara said. "Because he yet thinks this is about strength. It is not. It is about will. About who can hold their ground when the shadows close in. That is what he has never understood."

Ada let out a long, trembling breath. The energy from The Channel was flowing through her now, not harshly but like an unseen current, steady and alive. It filled every space fear had once occupied.

For a long moment, the room was silent save for the faint hum of magic. The fog pressed harder against the windows, and Ada turned toward it. The darkness beyond the glass was no longer empty; it shimmered faintly, alive with movement. The curtain between worlds was thinning. She could feel it. Tomorrow night, it would give way completely.

The mark upon her arm flared again, casting gold light across her face. She could feel its warmth sinking deep into her bones. "And I will be ready," she said softly.

Kito lifted his head, his amber eyes catching the light. He let out a single, low bark, short and certain, a promise.

Ada smiled faintly and drew the cloak tighter around her shoulders. The air had grown even colder, but she no longer felt its bite. She felt something else instead—the steady thrum of her ancestors, the whisper of the sea beyond, and the faint vibration of The Channel beneath her hand, waiting.

"I come for you, Malrik," she said quietly, her voice barely more than a breath. "And this time, you shall hear my bell."

As she spoke, the candles flared suddenly brighter, flooding the small cottage with gold light. For an instant, Ada thought she saw shapes moving within the glow, faces of those who had come before her, watching, waiting, proud.

The light lingered for a few heartbeats, then dimmed back to normal. The hum faded. The room settled.

Ada sank slowly to the floor beside Kito, leaning back against the bed. Exhaustion struck her all at once, the kind that ran deeper than the body. But beneath the weariness, she felt calm. Resolved.

Outside, the fog thickened until the world beyond the cottage vanished entirely. The air felt heavy with promise, with the weight of something vast approaching.

Kito curled closer, his warmth steady against her side. Ada closed her eyes. For the first time in years, her dreams were clear, filled not with fear or guilt but with light, voices, and the faint toll of a bell that no longer sounded like doom.

It sounded like calling.

Tomorrow, she would answer.

Chapter 10:

Breaking the Curse

The next night came with no stars and no moon, as if the sky itself had turned away from what was about to unfold. Ada stood in her cottage, dressed in the Gray cloak that shimmered like water in the candlelight. The Channel lay spread before her on the table, its dark wood gleaming with expectation. Kito sat beside her, his amber eyes reflecting the flickering flames.

She had not eaten since dawn. Her stomach felt hollow, but food would not stay down. The mark on her arm pulsed steadily, warm beneath the cloth of her sleeve, counting the hours like a second heartbeat. Outside, the fog pressed against every window, thick as wool, waiting.

"It's time," she whispered.

Kito rose to his feet, his massive form casting long shadows across the walls. He moved to the door and looked back at her, his gaze steady and sure. Ada nodded and placed her hands on The Channel for the last time in the world of the living.

The wooden plank grew warm beneath her fingers. The symbols around the board's edge began to glow, one by one, until the entire surface pulsed with golden light. The air in the cottage shimmered, and Ada felt the familiar presence of the spirits gathering around her.

"We are with you," came Elara's voice, soft and certain. "Every step of the way."

"The door is opening," added Marcus Gray. "Step through with courage, child. You carry all our hopes."

The golden light spread outward from the board, flowing across the table and onto the floor. Where it touched, the wooden planks became transparent, revealing not the ground beneath the cottage but something else entirely. A vast, dark landscape stretched out below them, shrouded in mist and shadow. Moorlow.

Ada took a deep breath and stepped forward. The moment her foot touched the light, the world changed around her.

The cottage walls faded like smoke. The candles guttered out, but the darkness that followed was not empty. It was alive, pressing against her skin with cold fingers that seemed to search for weakness. The air was thick and heavy, tasting of salt and old graves. Every breath felt like drinking fog.

Kito appeared beside her, his form more solid here than it had been in the living world. His fur held a faint luminescence, and his eyes burned like twin stars in the gloom. He pressed close to her side as they both looked out over the realm of the Bellringer.

Moorlow stretched before them like a twisted mirror of the world they had left behind. The landscape rolled in gentle hills, but the grass beneath their feet was gray and brittle. Trees rose from the mist, their branches bare and reaching toward a sky that held no sun, only a dim, sourceless light that seemed to come from everywhere and nowhere.

And everywhere, moving through the shadows like lost children, were the souls of the missing.

Ada's heart clenched as she saw them. Hundreds of figures drifted through the gray landscape, their forms pale and translucent. She recognized faces from Lowmere: Tam

Fletcher walking aimlessly near a withered oak, Sarah Whitmore sitting by a stream that held no water, old Henrik staring at the empty sky with hollow eyes.

They turned toward her as she passed, their faces lighting with something that might have been hope. But they did not speak. They could not, Ada realized. Not yet. Not until she reached the heart of this place and faced the one who held them prisoner.

"Stay close," she whispered to Kito, though she knew he would never leave her side.

They began to walk deeper into Moorlow, following a path that seemed to form beneath their feet with each step. The trapped souls followed at a distance, a silent procession of the lost and forgotten. Their whispers filled the air like wind through dry leaves, all saying the same thing: *Free us. Please, free us.*

The farther they walked, the stranger the landscape became. Time seemed to flow differently here, sometimes fast, sometimes slow, sometimes not at all. Ada saw ruins of buildings that had never existed in the living world, monuments to forgotten sorrows and abandoned dreams. The very air shimmered with malevolent energy, and she could feel eyes watching her from every shadow.

But she did not falter. The mark on her arm grew brighter with each step, casting a protective glow that pushed back the darkness. The Gray cloak flowed around her like liquid silver, turning away the grasping tendrils of shadow that tried to snare her feet. And always, the presence of her ancestors walked beside her, their voices whispering encouragement in the growing dark.

At last, they reached the heart of Moorlow.

It was a vast amphitheater carved from black stone, its walls rising impossibly high into the mist-shrouded sky. At its center stood a tower that seemed to be made of solidified shadow, its surface writhing and shifting like a living thing. And before the tower, seated on a throne of bones and coral, was Malrik himself.

Ada's breath caught in her throat. She had expected him to be terrible, but nothing could have prepared her for the reality. He was tall and gaunt, his form shifting between solid flesh and drifting smoke. His face was beautiful and horrible at once, with features that seemed carved from marble but eyes that held the depth of the ocean's darkest trenches. Around him, the air itself seemed to bend and twist, as if reality could not quite decide what he was.

When he saw her approach, Malrik smiled. The expression was worse than any snarl would have been.

"So," he said, his voice echoing from every stone in the amphitheater, "the little marked child has come to me at last. How precious. How brave. How utterly foolish."

Ada stepped forward, Kito at her side. The trapped souls gathered behind them, their forms becoming more solid as they drew closer to their captor. She could feel their pain, their longing for freedom, pressing against her mind like a physical weight.

"I've come to end this," she said, her voice carrying clearly through the still air.

Malrik laughed, the sound like breaking glass and screaming wind. "End this? Child, you have no idea what 'this' truly is. You think I am some simple monster to be slain, some curse to be broken with good intentions and righteous anger?"

He rose from his throne, and as he did, his form grew larger, more terrible. Shadows poured from him like smoke from a fire, filling the amphitheater with writhing darkness.

"I am the bargain your ancestors made," he continued, his voice growing louder with each word. "I am the price they agreed to pay. I am woven into the very foundation of your precious town, bound to its stones and its soil and its people. Destroy me, and Lowmere dies with me. Is that what you want, little hero? To save everyone by killing them?"

For a moment, doubt crept into Ada's heart. What if he was right? What if breaking the curse would destroy everything she was trying to protect?

But then she heard her grandfather's voice, clear and strong: "He lies, Ada. The bargain was made in desperation, not wisdom. It can be unmade the same way."

And Elara's voice followed: "You are not here to destroy, child. You are here to heal."

Ada felt the mark on her arm flare with warmth, and suddenly she understood. This was not about breaking something. It was about fixing what had been broken long ago.

"You're wrong," she said, stepping closer to the throne. "The bargain was flawed from the beginning. My ancestors were desperate, terrified people who made a deal they didn't understand with a creature they couldn't comprehend. But they were also wise enough to build a way out. They built me."

Malrik's smile faltered. "Impossible. The bloodlines are bound to me. You belong to me, marked one. Your very soul bears my seal."

"No," Ada said firmly. "This mark doesn't belong to you. It never did."

She pulled back her sleeve, revealing the bell-shaped outline that pulsed with golden light. But as she watched, the mark began to change. The edges softened, the harsh lines becoming flowing curves. It was still a bell, but now it looked like something else as well—a flower opening to the sun, a doorway standing ajar, a hand extended in welcome rather than warning.

"It belongs to them," Ada continued, gesturing to the gathered souls. "To the lost, the forgotten, the taken. And I'm here to give it back."

Malrik snarled and lunged forward, his form shifting into something bestial and terrible. Claws of shadow reached for Ada's throat, but Kito was faster. The great hyena leaped between them, his own form blazing with protective light as he caught the Bellringer's attack.

The collision sent shockwaves through the amphitheater. Stone cracked, mist swirled, and the trapped souls cried out in voices that were finally their own. Kito and Malrik tumbled across the black stone, a whirlwind of shadow and light, fang and claw.

Ada reached into her coat and pulled out The Channel's components, the plank, the bone tokens, the cards marked with ancient symbols. She spread them on the ground before her and knelt, placing her hands on the familiar board.

Immediately, power flowed through her. Not just from The Channel, but from every soul in the amphitheater. They were all connected now, all part of the same great plan that her ancestors had begun generations ago.

"I call on the power of the founding families," she said, her voice rising above the sounds of battle. "I call on the blood of the Thornes, the wisdom of the Grays, the strength of the Blackwoods, the courage of the Merrows."

The mark on her arm blazed brighter, and lights appeared in response throughout the amphitheater. Every trapped soul bore a mark now, faint but growing stronger, symbols that showed their connection to the town they had been stolen from, the lives they had been forced to leave behind.

Malrik broke away from Kito with a roar of fury. The hyena lay motionless on the stone, his breathing shallow, dark liquid staining his golden fur. Ada's heart clenched with terror and rage.

"You killed them!" she screamed, power crackling around her like lightning. "All of them! For what? For your hunger? For your pleasure?"

"For survival!" Malrik snarled back. "For existence! Do you think I chose this, little fool? Do you think I wanted to become what I am?"

For the first time, Ada heard something other than malice in his voice. Pain. Loneliness. Ancient, crushing sorrow.

"Then let it end," she said softly. "Let us both be free."

She pressed her hands harder against The Channel, calling on every lesson her ancestors had taught her, every scrap of power that flowed in her blood. The board blazed with light so bright it turned the black stone white, and the symbols carved into its surface rose into the air like living things.

The trapped souls began to sing.

It started with just one voice, Tam Fletcher, clear and strong. Then Sarah joined him, and Henrik, and all the others. Their voices rose in harmony, not the desperate whispers of the lost but the joyful chorus of the found. The sound filled the amphitheater, spilled out across the gray landscape of Moorlow, and began to change everything it touched.

Grass sprouted green where the music fell. Flowers bloomed in the withered trees. The sourceless light in the sky grew warmer, brighter, touched with gold instead of gray.

Malrik staggered backward, his form flickering like a candle in the wind. "No," he gasped. "No, this cannot be. I am eternal. I am necessary. Without me, the sea will claim them all."

"The sea was never the enemy," Ada said, understanding flooding through her like sunrise. "You were just afraid of it, like they were. But fear is not a foundation. It's a prison."

She stood, still connected to The Channel but no longer bound to the ground. Light poured from her mark, from her eyes, from her very soul. She was not Ada the outcast anymore, not Ada the cursed. She was Ada the bridge-builder, Ada the peacemaker, Ada the one who could stand between two worlds and help them remember how to speak to each other.

"I offer you another bargain," she said to Malrik. "Not one born from desperation, but from understanding. The souls you've held, let them choose. Let them decide if they want to stay in Moorlow or return to the living world. And you, you can choose too. Stay here as a guardian instead of a jailer, or find your own way home to whatever realm you came from. But the forced feeding ends now."

Malrik stared at her, his terrible face cycling through emotions too complex to name. Around them, the trapped souls continued to sing, their voices transforming the very fabric of his realm.

"You would trust me with such a choice?" he asked finally.

"I would trust everyone with choice," Ada replied. "That's what was missing from the original bargain. No one chose freely. It was all fear and desperation and threats. But choice, real choice, that's what makes a bond strong."

For a long moment, the Bellringer was silent. Then, slowly, his monstrous form began to shift and change. The claws retracted, the shadows pulled back, and what remained was still tall and strange but no longer terrible. He looked almost human, if humans could be made of starlight and sea foam.

"I remember," he said, his voice soft with wonder. "I remember what I was before the hunger took hold. Before the fear. I was... a guide. A keeper of thresholds. I helped souls find their way between worlds."

"You could be that again," Ada said gently.

Malrik—no, the being who had once been more than Malrik—nodded slowly. "And the town? Lowmere?"

"Will choose its own relationship with the sea," Ada said. "As it should have from the beginning."

The light from her mark spread outward, touching every soul in the amphitheater. One by one, they stepped forward, and one by one, they made their choice. Some, like Tam, chose to return to the world of the living, not as they had been, but as spirits who could visit their loved ones and offer comfort. Others, like old Henrik, chose to stay in Moorlow, which was transforming around them into something beautiful, a place of rest and reflection, where souls could heal from the traumas of life before moving on to whatever came next.

And some, like the creature who had been Malrik, chose something new entirely. He became the guardian of the threshold, the keeper of the way between worlds, helping souls pass safely in both directions as they chose their own destinies.

The amphitheater crumbled as its purpose ended, the black stones dissolving into flower petals that blew away on a wind that smelled of salt and spring rain. The tower of shadow collapsed into light, and where it had stood, a fountain sprang up, its water clear and sweet.

Ada felt herself growing lighter, the boundaries of her body becoming less distinct. She was still herself, but she was also something more, a living bridge between the worlds, a keeper of the peace that had been so long in coming.

She turned to look for Kito and found him standing beside her, his wounds healed, his golden fur shining like the sun. But he was different too, she realized. The ancient bond that had tied him to her bloodline was loosening, freeing him to choose his own path as well.

"Will you stay?" she asked him.

He nuzzled her hand once, gently, then stepped back. His form shimmered and changed, and Ada saw him as he truly was, not just a hyena, but a spirit of protection and guidance, freed now to help any who needed him, not just the descendants of a single family.

"Thank you," she whispered. "For everything."

He barked once, a sound full of joy and farewell, then bounded away across the transformed landscape of Moorlow, already moving to help other souls find their way.

Ada smiled and turned back toward the world of the living. The Channel still lay on the ground where she had left it, but it looked different now. Instead of dark wood carved with mysterious symbols, it was simple, clean, welcoming. Anyone could use it, she realized. Not just those marked by ancient bloodlines, but anyone who needed to speak with those they had lost.

She picked it up and walked toward the shimmer in the air that marked the way home.

The crossing back was gentler than the journey into Moorlow had been. Ada found herself standing in her cottage as dawn light streamed through the windows, The Channel once again on her kitchen table. But everything felt different. Lighter. Free.

She walked to her window and looked out over Lowmere. The fog was lifting, and for the first time in generations, she could see all the way to the horizon. The sea sparkled in the morning sun, and fishing boats dotted its surface, not fleeing from danger, but working in harmony with the waves.

A knock at her door made her turn. She opened it to find a crowd of townspeople standing in her garden, their faces curious rather than fearful. At their front stood Mrs. Carven, who looked up at Ada with eyes that held no blame, only wonder.

"The bell didn't toll last night," Mrs. Carven said. "For the first time in living memory, the New Moon passed without the thirteenth bell. What happened?"

Ada smiled and held up her arm. Where the bell-shaped mark had been, there was now only smooth skin, unmarked, unburdened, free.

"We all chose differently," she said simply.

The crowd murmured among themselves, but it was not the fearful whispering of old. It was the sound of people beginning to hope, beginning to believe that change was not only possible but already here.

Over the following days, Lowmere transformed. The constant fear that had gripped the town for generations began to fade. People ventured out on New Moon nights. Fishermen sailed farther from shore. Children played in the streets without looking over their shoulders.

And sometimes, on quiet evenings when the sea was calm, families would gather around The Channel, which Ada kept in the town square now, available to all, and speak with loved ones who had passed on. Not because they were trapped or summoned, but because love was stronger than death, and some connections were meant to last.

The curse was broken, but more than that, it was transformed into something beautiful. A gift freely given instead of a price forcibly extracted. A bridge between worlds instead of a wall.

Ada still lived in her cottage on the cliff, but she was no longer alone. Visitors came daily, some seeking comfort, some offering friendship, all recognizing her as the one who had given them back their freedom. She was no longer the marked child, the cursed survivor, the outcast on the edge of town.

She was simply Ada, the bridge-builder, the peacemaker, the one who had shown them all that even the darkest curses could be transformed by choice, understanding, and love. And on clear nights, when the moon was full and the sea was silver, she would sometimes see a familiar golden shape running along the shoreline—Kito, still protecting, still guiding, but free now to help anyone who needed him.

The thirteenth bell would never toll again. But if it had, its sound would no longer have been a call to death. It would have been a call to come home.